EARLY LESSONS. IN TWO VOLUMES. VOL. I

Published @ 2017 Trieste Publishing Pty Ltd

ISBN 9780649566716

Early Lessons. In Two Volumes. Vol. I by Maria Edgeworth

Edited by Trieste Publishing Pty Ltd.
 Cover @ 2017

www.triestepublishing.com

MARIA EDGEWORTH

EARLY LESSONS. IN TWO VOLUMES. VOL. I

 Trieste

EARLY LESSONS.

IN TWO VOLUMES.

BY MARIA EDGEWORTH.

SIXTH EDITION.

VOL. I.

CONTAINING

FRANK.

THE LITTLE DOG TRUSTY.

THE ORANGE MAN.

THE CHERRY ORCHARD.

LONDON:

PRINTED FOR R. HUNTER,

SUCCESSOR TO MR. JOHNSON, 72, ST. PAUL'S CHURCHYARD;

AND BALDWIN, CRADOCK, AND JOY,

PATERNOSTER ROW.

1818.

CHARLES WOOD, Printer,
Poppin's Court, Fleet Street, London.

DEDICATION.

TO

MY LITTLE BROTHER WILLIAM.

M. E.

FRANK.

———

THERE was a little boy, whose name
was Frank. He had a father and a
mother, who were very kind to him;
and he loved them; he liked to talk
to them, and he liked to walk with
them, and he liked to be with them.
He liked to do what they asked him
to do; and he took care not to do what
they desired him not to do. When
his father or mother said to him,
" Frank, shut the door," he ran directly, and shut the door. When they
said to him, " Frank, do not touch

that knife," he took his hands away from the knife, and did not touch it.— He was an obedient little boy.

One evening, when his father and mother were drinking tea, he was sitting under the tea-table; and he took hold of one of the legs of the table; and he tried to pull it towards himself; but he could not move it. He took hold of another leg of the table; and he found that he could not move it: but at last he took hold of one, which he found that he could move very easily; for this leg turned upon a hinge, and was not fixed, like the other legs. As he was drawing this leg of the table towards him, his mother said to him, " Frank, what are you doing?"

And he answered, " Mamma, I am playing with the leg of the table."

And his mother said, " What do you

mean by saying that you are playing with the leg of the table?"

And Frank said, " I mean, that I am pulling it towards me, mamma."

And his mother said, " Let it alone, my dear."

And Frank took his hands away from the leg of the table, and he let it alone; and he came from under the table; and he got up, and stood beside his mother: and he said, " Mamma, I come away from the leg of the table, that I may not think of touching it any more:" and his father and mother smiled.

And Frank said, " But mother, will you tell me why you bid me let it alone?"

" Yes, I will, my dear," said his mother; and she then moved some of the tea-cups and saucers to another table; and Frank's father put the tea-urn upon another table; and then

Frank's mother said to him, " Now, my dear Frank, go and push the leg of the table, as you did before."

And Frank pushed the leg of the table; and when he had pushed it a little way, he stopped, and looked up at his mother, and said, " I see part of the top of the table moving down towards my head, mamma; and, if I push this leg any farther back, I am afraid that part of 'the table will fall down upon my head and hurt me."

" I will hold up this part of the table, which is called the *leaf*," said his mother; " and I will not let it fall down upon your head.—Pull the leg of the table back as far as you can.", And Frank did as his mother desired him; and, when he had pulled it back as far as he could, his mother bid him come from under the table; and he did so: and she said, " Stand beside me, and look what happens when I let go this leaf of the table, which I am now holding."

And Frank said, " I know what will happen, I believe, mamma : it will fall ; for now, that I have pulled back the leg, there is nothing to hold it up but your hand."

Then his mother took away her hand, and the leaf of the table fell ; and Frank put his hand upon his head, and said, " Oh, mamma, that would have hurt me very much, if it had fallen upon my head — I am glad I was not under the table when the leaf fell — And now I believe I know the reason, mamma, why you asked me not to meddle with that leg of the table : because the leaf (is not that the name you told me?), the leaf would have fallen upon my head, and would have hurt me — Was not that the reason, mamma ?"

" That was one reason ; but I had some other reasons.—Try if you can find out what they were, Frank," said his mother.

And Frank looked at the table for a little while, and then answered, " I don't know any other reasons, mamma;" but, as he was saying these words, he saw his mother turn her head towards the table, upon which she had put the cups and saucers.

" Oh, now, mamma," said Frank, " I know what you mean.—If those cups and saucers had been upon this leaf of the table, they would have slid down when it fell, and they would have been broken.—And the urn, too, mamma, would have come tumbling down ; and perhaps the top of the urn would have come off ; and then all the hot water would have come running out, and would have wet the room, and would have scalded me, if I had been under it—I am very glad, mamma, that I did as you bid me."

ONE day, Frank's mother took him out to walk with her in the fields; and he saw flowers of different colours, blue, red, yellow, and purple; and he asked his mother, whether he might gather some of these flowers.

She answered, " Yes, my dear; you may gather as many of these flowers as you please."

Then Frank ran, and gathered several flowers; and, in one corner of this field, upon a bank, he saw some blue-bells; and he liked blue-bells; and he ran and gathered them; and, in the next field, he saw a great number of purple flowers, which he thought looked very pretty; and he got over the stile, and went into the next field, and went close up to the purple flowers: they had yellow in the middle of them; and they grew upon a plant, which had a great number of green leaves.

As Frank was pulling some of the purple flowers, he shook the green leaves; and he saw amongst them several little green balls, which looked like very small apples. Frank wished to taste them; and he was just going to pull one from the stalk, when he recollected, that his mother had not given him leave to have them; and he ran back to his mother, and said, " Mamma, may I have some of those nice little apples?" and he pointed to the plants on which the purple flowers grew.

His mother answered, " I do not see
any apples, my dear."

" You will see them, mamma, if
you will come a little closer to them,"
said Frank ; and he took his mother by
the hand, and led her to the plants,
and showed her the little green balls,
which he thought were apples.

" My dear little boy," said his mother, " these are not apples ; these
things are not good to be eaten ; they
are poisonous ; they would have made
you sick, if you had eaten them."

" I am glad," said Frank, " that I
did not taste them. But may I have
one of them for a ball ? "

" No, my dear," said his mother,
" do not meddle with any of them."

Frank walked on, in the path,
beside his mother ; and he did not
meddle with any of the little green

balls. And he saw, at a little distance from him, a boy, who was digging: and when he came near to this boy, Frank saw, that he was digging up some of the plants that bore the pretty purple flowers ; and Frank said, " Mamma, why does this boy dig up these things?—Is he going to throw them away ? "

And Frank's mother said, " Look, and you will see what part of them he keeps, and what part of them he throws away."

And Frank looked; and he saw that the boy pulled off some of the brown and white round roots of the plant; and he put these roots into a basket. The green part of the plant, and the purple flowers, and the green balls, which Frank mistook for apples, he saw that the boy threw away.

And Frank said to his mother, " What are those roots in the basket?"

His mother said, " Look at them; and try if you can find out—You have eaten roots like them—You often see roots like these at dinner."

" I do not remember," said Frank, " ever having seen such dirty things as these at dinner."

" They are washed and boiled before you see them at dinner; and then they look white," said his mother.

Frank looked again at the roots, which were in the basket; and he said, " Mamma, I think that they are potatoes."

" Yes, my dear, they are potatoes," said his mother; and then Frank and his mother went on a little farther; and they came to a large shady tree; and Frank's mother sat down upon a bank under the shade of this tree, to cool and rest herself; for she was hot and tired.

Frank was not tired; therefore, he did not sit down: but he amused himself with trying to reach some of the branches of the tree, which hung over his head.

He jumped up as high as he could, to catch them; but he found, that several, which he thought he could reach, he could not touch, even when he stretched out his hand and arm, and stood on tiptoe.

At last, he saw a bough, which hung lower than the other boughs; and he jumped up, and caught hold of it; and he held it down, that he might look at the leaves of the tree.

" Mamma," said he, " these leaves are not like the leaves of the tree, which is near the hall-door, at home — You told me the name of that tree ; that tree is called a beech. — What is the name of this tree?"

" This tree is called a horse-chesnut-tree."

" Mamma," said Frank ; " here are little green balls upon this tree ; they are something like those I saw upon the potatoes — I won't meddle with them : they have prickles upon them."

And Frank's mother said, " You may gather some of these little balls, my dear; these are not of the same sort as those you saw on the potatoe-plants. — These are not poisonous: these are called horse-chesnuts — The prickles are not very sharp — You may break them off."

" How many of these horse-chesnuts may I gather, mamma?" said Frank.

" You may gather four of them, my dear," said his mother; and Frank gathered four of the horse-chesnuts — Then he let go the bough; and he sat down upon the bank, beside his mother, to examine his horse-chesnuts.—His mother broke one of them open for him—The inside of the green husk was white and soft ; and in the middle of this white, soft substance, there lay a smooth, shining kernel, of the colour of mahogany.

" Is it good to eat, mamma?" said Frank— May I taste it?"

"You may taste it, if you please, my dear," said his mother; " but I do not think, that you will like it; for that brown skin has a bitter taste; and I do not think the inside of it is agree-

able; but you may taste it, if you like
it."

Frank tasted it, and he did not like
the bitter of the outside; and he said,
" Mamma, I will always take care to
ask you, before I meddle with things or
taste them, because you know more
than I do: and you can tell me whether they are good for me or not."

Frank's mother having now rested
herself, got up from her seat; and she
walked home; and Frank carried his
three horse-chesnuts home with him —
He did not put them into his mouth,
because he had learned that they tasted
bitter; but he used them as balls; and
he rolled them along the floor, when
he got into the house; and he was very
happy playing with them.

ANOTHER day, Frank went out to walk with his mother; and he came to a gate, that was painted green: and he stopped at the gate, and looked between the rails of it: and he saw a pretty garden, with several beds of flowers in it; and there were nice clean gravel-walks between these flower beds, and all round the garden — And against the walls of the garden there were plum trees, and cherry-trees; and the cherries and plums looked as if they were quite ripe.

And Frank called to his mother, who was a little way off; and he said, " Mamma, come and look at this pretty garden — I wish I might open this gate, and go in and walk in it."

" My dear," said his mother, " you must not open the gate — This garden does not belong to me; and I cannot give you leave to walk in it."

There was a man, nailing up a net, over a cherry-tree, in this garden; and he came to the gate, and opened it, and said, " Will you walk in, ma'am? This garden belongs to me; and you shall be very welcome to walk in it."— And Frank's mother thanked the man; and she then turned to Frank, and said, " If I take you with me, Frank, to walk in this garden, you must take care not to meddle with any thing in it."— And Frank said that he would not meddle with any thing in the garden; and his mother took him into it.

As he walked along the gravel-walks, he looked at every thing; but he did not touch any thing.

A very sweet smell came from two beds of pinks and carnations; and he stood at a little distance from them, looking at them; and the man to whom the garden belonged, said to him, "Walk down this narrow path, master, between the beds, and you'll see my carnations better."

And Frank answered, "I should like to come down that narrow path; but I am afraid of coming, because the skirts of my coat, I am afraid, will brush against the flowers——I saw your coat, just now, sir, hit against the top of a flower; and it broke it."

Frank's mother smiled, and said, "I am glad, my dear little boy, that you are so careful not to do mischief."

Frank did not tread upon any of the borders; and the person to whom the garden belonged, who was a gardener, said to his mother, "I hope, whenever you come this way again, ma'am, you'll walk in this garden of mine, and bring this little gentleman with you; for I am sure, by what I see of him now, that he will not do me any mischief."

The gardener told Frank the names of several flowers; and he showed him the seeds of some of these flowers; and he showed Frank how these seeds should be sowed in the ground.

And whilst the gardener was showing Frank how to sow the seeds of minionette, he heard a noise at the gate; and he looked, and he saw a boy, who was shaking the gate, and trying to get in; but the gate was locked, and the boy could not open it; and the boy called to the gardener, and said, " Let me in; let me in—Won't you let me in?"

But the gardener answered, " No—I will not let you come in, sir, I assure you; for when I did let you in, yesterday, you meddled with my flowers, and you ate some of my cherries—I do not choose to let you in here again—I do not choose to let a dishonest boy into my garden, who meddles with what does not belong to him."

This boy looked very much ashamed, and very sorry, that he might not come into the pretty garden; and he stood at the gate for some time; but, when he found that the gardener would not let him in, he went slowly away.

A little while afterwards, Frank asked his mother, why she did not gather some of the pinks in this garden; and his mother answered, " Because they are not mine; and I must not meddle with what does not belong to me."

" I did not know, till now, mamma," said Frank, "that *you* must not meddle with what does not belong to you—I thought that people only said to little boys—*You must not meddle with what does not belong to you."*

" My dear," said Frank's mother, " neither men, nor women, nor children, should meddle with what does not belong to them — Little children do not know this till it is told to them."

" And, mamma," said Frank, " what is the reason that men, women, and children, should not meddle with what does not belong to them ?"

Frank's mother answered, " I cannot explain all the reasons to you yet, my dear—But should you like that any body should take flowers out of the little garden you have at home?"

" No, mamma, I should not."

" And did you not see that the boy, who just now came to this green gate, was prevented by the gardener from coming into this garden, because, yesterday, the boy took flowers and fruit, which did not belong to him — *You*, Frank, have not meddled with any of these flowers, or this fruit; and you know the gardener said, that he would let you come in here again, whenever I like to bring you with me."

" I am very glad of that, mamma," said Frank; " for I like to walk in this pretty garden; and I will take care not to meddle with any thing, that does not belong to me."

Then Frank's mother said, " It is time that we should go home." And Frank thanked the gardener for letting him walk in his garden, and for showing him how to sow seeds in the ground; and Frank went home with his mother."

A few days after Frank had been
with his mother to walk in the garden,
that had the green gate, his mother
said to him, " Frank, put on your hat
and come with me—I am going to the
garden in which we walked two or
three days ago."

Frank was very glad to hear this—
He put on his hat in an instant, and
followed his mother, jumping and
singing as he went along.

When they were in the fields, which
led to the garden with the green gate,
Frank ran on before his mother—He
came to a stile: a boy of about Frank's
size was sitting upon the uppermost
step of the stile. He had a hat upon
his knees, in which there were some
nuts ; and the boy was picking the
white kernel of a nut out of its shell.

When the boy saw Frank, he said

to him, "Do you want to get over this stile?"

And Frank answered, "Yes, I do."

The boy then got up from the step of the stile on which he was sitting; and he jumped down, and walked on, that he might make room for Frank to get over the stile.

Frank and his mother got over the stile; and, in the path in the next field, at a little distance from the stile, Frank saw a fine bunch of nuts.

"Mamma," said Frank, "I think these nuts belong to that little boy, who was sitting upon the stile, with nuts in his hat: perhaps he dropped them, and did not know it—May I pick them up, and run after the little boy, and give them to him?"

His mother said, "Yes, my dear;

and I will go back with you to the boy."
—So Frank picked up the nuts; and he
and his mother went back; and he
called to the little boy, who stopped
when he heard him call.

And as soon as Frank came near to
him, and had breath to speak, he said
to the boy, " Here are some nuts,
which I believe are yours — I found
them in the path, near that stile."

" Thank you," said the boy; " they
are mine — I dropped them there; and
I am much obliged to you for bringing
them back to me."

Frank saw that the boy was glad to
have his nuts again; and Frank was
glad that he had found them, and that
he had returned them to the person to
whom they belonged.

Frank then went on with his mother;
and they came to the garden with the

green gate. The gardener was tying the
pinks and carnations to white sticks,
which he stuck in the ground near
them.—He did this to prevent the
flowers from hanging down in the dirt,
and from being broken by the wind.

Frank told his mother, that he
thought he could tie up some of these
flowers, and that he should like to try
to do it.

She asked the gardener, if he would
let Frank try to help him.

The gardener said he would; and he
gave Frank a bundle of sticks, and
some strings made of bass mat: and
Frank stuck the sticks in the ground,
and tied the pinks and carnations to
them; and he said, " Mamma, I am of
some use;" and he was happy whilst
he was employed in this manner.

After the flowers were all tied up,

the gardener went to the cherry-tree, which was nailed up against the wall; and he took down the net, which was spread over it.

Frank asked his mother, why this net had been spread over it.

She told him, that it was to prevent the birds from pecking at and eating the cherries.

The cherries looked very ripe, and the gardener began to gather them.

Frank asked, whether he might help him to gather some of the cherries.

His mother said, " Yes; I think the gardener will trust you to gather his cherries, because he has seen that you have not meddled with any of his things without his leave."

The gardener said, that he would trust him; and Frank was glad; and he gathered all the cherries, that he could reach, that were ripe.

The gardener desired, that he would not gather any that were not ripe; and his mother showed Frank a ripe and an unripe cherry, that he might know the difference between them; and she asked the gardener, if he would let Frank taste these two cherries, that he might know the difference in the taste.

"If you please, ma'am," said the gardener; and Frank tasted the cherries, and he found that the ripe cherry was sweet, and the unripe cherry was sour.

The gardener told him, that the cherries, which were now unripe, would grow ripe in a few days, if they were let to hang upon the tree, and if the sun shone.

And Frank said, " Mamma, if you

let me come with you here again in a few days, I will look at these cherries, that I may see whether they do grow ripe."

Frank took care to gather only the cherries that were ripe; and when he had filled the basket into which the gardener asked him to put them, the gardener picked out five or six bunches of the ripest cherries; and he offered them to Frank.

" May I have them, mamma?" said Frank.

His mother said, " Yes, you may, my dear."

Then he took them; and he thanked the gardener for giving them to him; and, after this, he and his mother left the garden, and returned towards home.

He asked his mother to eat some of

the cherries; and she took one bunch; and she said that she liked them.

" And I will keep another bunch for papa," said Frank, " because I know he likes cherries."

And Frank ate all the rest of the cherries, except the bunch which he kept for his father; and he said, " I wish, mother, you would give me a little garden, and some minionette-seeds to sow in it."

She answered, " This is not the time of year in which minionette-seed should be sown: the seeds will not grow, if you sow them now—We must wait till spring."

Frank was going to say, " How many months will it be between this time and spring;" but he forgot what he was going to say, because he saw a boy in the field in which they were walking, who had something made of white paper in his hand, which was fluttering in the wind.

"What is that, mamma?" said Frank.

"It is a paper kite, my dear," said his mother; "you shall see the boy flying this kite, if you please."

"I do not know what you mean by flying the kite, mamma," said Frank.

"Look at what the boy is doing, and you will see."

Frank looked, and he saw the paper kite blown by the wind; and it mounted up higher than the trees, and went higher and higher, till it seemed to touch the clouds, and till it appeared no larger than a little black spot; and at last, Frank lost sight of it entirely.

The boy, who had been flying the kite, now ran up to the place where

Frank was standing; and Frank saw that he was the same boy to whom he had returned the nuts.

The boy held one end of a string in his hand; and the other end of the string, Frank's mother told him, was fastend to the kite.

The boy pulled the string towards him, and wound it up on a bit of wood; and Frank saw the paper kite again, coming downwards; and it fell lower and lower, and lower; and, at last, it fell to the ground.

The boy, to whom it belonged, went to fetch it; and Frank's mother said, "Now we must make haste, and go home."

Frank followed his mother, asking her several questions about the kite; and he did not perceive, that he had not his bunch of cherries in his hand,

till he was near home — When his mother said, " There is your father coming to meet us," Frank cried, " Oh,
mamma ! my cherries, the nice bunch
of cherries that I kept to give him — I
have dropped them — I have lost them—
I am very sorry for it — May I run back
to look for them ? — I think I dropped
them whilst I was looking at the kite—
May I go back to that field, and look
for them ?"

" No, my dear," said his mother;
" it is just dinner time."

Frank was sorry for this; and he
looked back, towards the field where
he lost his cherries; and he saw the
boy with the kite in his hand, running
very fast across the field nearest to
him.

" I think he seems to be running to

us, mamma," said Frank—" Will you wait one minute ?"

His mother stopped, and the boy ran up to them, quite out of breath — He held his kite in one hand ; and in his other hand he held Frank's bunch of cherries.

" Oh, my cherries ! thank you for bringing them to me," said Frank.

" You seem to be as glad as I was, when you brought me my nuts," said the boy—" you dropped the cherries in the field where I was flying my kite —I knew they were yours, because I saw them in your hand when you were looking at my kite."

Frank thanked the boy again for returning them to him ; and his mother also said to the boy, " Thank you, my little honest boy."

"I was honest, mamma, when I returned his nuts to him; and he was honest when he returned my cherries—I liked him for being honest; and he liked me for being honest—I will always be honest about every thing, as well as about nuts."—Then Frank ran to meet his father, with the ripe bunch of cherries, and gave them to him; and his father liked them very much.

———

THE evening after Frank had seen the boy flying a kite, he asked his father, if he would be so good as to give him a kite.

"My dear," said his father, "I am busy now; I am writing a letter; and I cannot think about kites now—Do not talk to me about kites when I am busy."

When his father had finished writing his letter, he folded it up, and took up some sealing-wax to seal it; and Frank watched the sealing-wax, as it was melted by the heat of the candle. He saw, that his father let some of the melted sealing-wax drop upon the paper; and then he pressed the seal down upon the wax, which had dropped upon the paper, and which was then soft.

When the seal was taken up, Frank saw, that there was the figure of the head of a man upon the wax; and he looked at the bottom of the seal; and he said, " This is the same head that there is upon the wax, only this on the seal goes inwards, and that on the wax comes outwards."

He touched the wax upon which the seal had been pressed; and he felt that

it was now cold and hard; and he said,
" Papa, are you busy now ? "

And his father said that he was not
busy.

And Frank asked him, if he would
drop some more wax on a bit of paper,
and press the seal down upon it.

" Yes," said his father; " you were
not troublesome to me, when I said that
I was busy— Now I have leisure to
attend to you, my dear."

His father then took out of a drawer
three different seals; and he sealed
three different letters with these, and
let Frank see him drop the wax upon
the paper, and let Frank press down
the seals upon the soft wax.

" Papa, will you give me leave to
try if I can do it myself?" said Frank.

" My dear," said his mother, " I do
not like that you should meddle with

candles or with fire, lest you should set your clothes on fire and burn yourself, as many children of your age have done, when no one has been present to help them."

" But papa," said Frank, " I never meddle with candles or fire, when you or mamma are not in the room."

" Then now we are present you may try what you wish to do; but I advise you to take care," said his mother, " not to let any of the melted wax drop upon your hands; for it will burn you if you do."

Frank was in a great hurry to melt the wax—His mother called to him, and said—" Gently, Frank, or you will let the wax drop upon your hand and burn yourself."

But he said, " Oh, no, mamma; it will not burn me."

And just after he had said this, a drop of the melted sealing-wax fell upon the fore-finger of his hand, and burned him; and he squeezed his finger as hard as he could to try to stop the feeling of pain—" It hurts me very much, mamma!—I wish I had minded what you said to me—But I will not cry—I will bear it well."

" You do bear it well," said his father; " shake hands with me, with the hand that is not burnt."

A few minutes afterwards, Frank said, that he did not feel the pain any longer; and he asked his father, if he would give him leave to have the sealing-wax again, and to try whether he could not make such a seal as he had seen upon his father's letter, without burning himself—" You did not burn yourself, papa," said Frank; " and if I

take care and do it as you did, I shall
not burn myself—May I try again?"

"Yes, my dear," said his father;
"and I am glad to see, that you wish
to *try again*, though you have had a
little pain."

His father showed him, once more,
how to hold the wax to the candle, and
how to drop it, when melting, upon the
paper, without burning himself.

And Frank succeeded very well, this
time, and made a good impression from
the seal; and he showed it to his mother.

"Is not it *a good seal*, mamma?"
said he. "I took care not to hold the
wax this time as I did the last, when I
burned myself."

"Yes," said his mother, "I dare
say you remember how you held it
when you burned yourself."

" Oh, yes.; *that* I do, mamma : the pain makes me remember it, I believe."

" And I dare say you remember how you held the wax when you made this pretty seal."

" Oh, yes, mamma, *that* I do; and I shall remember to do it the same way the next time."

" You have been rewarded for your patience by having succeeded in making this seal; and you were punished for your carelessness, by having burned your fore-finger."

FRANK remembered, that his father desired him not to talk to him about kites when he was busy, and, though Frank was very eager to have a kite, he waited till he saw that his father was neither reading nor writing, nor talking to any body — Then he said, "Papa, I believe you are not busy now — Will you give me a kite?"

" I have not a kite, ready made, in my house," replied his father; " but I will show you how to make one; and I will give you some paper, and some paste, and some wood, to make it of." —Then his father gave him three large sheets of paper; and his mother rang the bell, and desired the servant would order the cook to make some paste.

And Frank asked his mother, how the cook made paste, and what she would make it of.

His mother took him by the hand, and said, " You shall see;" and she took Frank down stairs with her, into the kitchen, where he had never been before; and she staid with him whilst he looked at the manner in which the cook made the paste.

"What is that white powder, mamma, which the cook is taking up in her hands?" said Frank.

" It is called flour, my dear—You may take some of it in your hand; and you may taste it."

" Where does it come from, mamma?"

" From corn, my dear—You have seen corn growing in the fields; and when we walk out again into a field, where there is corn, if you will put me in mind, I will show you the part of the plant from which flour is made."

"Made, mamma! how is it made?"

" It is ground in a mill—But I cannot explain to you now, what I mean by that—When you see a mill, you will know."

" I should like to see a mill," said Frank, " now, this minute."

" But I cannot show it to you, Frank, now, this minute," said his mother; " besides, you came here to see how paste was made; and you had better attend to that now."

Frank attended: and he saw how paste was made . . . .

. . . . . . And when the paste was made, it was left upon a plate to cool.

Frank, as soon as it was cool enough to be used, took it to his father, and asked him, if he might now begin to make his kite; but his father said, " My dear, I cannot find two slips of wood for you; and you cannot well make your kite without them: but I am going to the carpenter's; and I can get such bits as I want from him — If you wish to come, you may come with me."

Frank said, that he should like to go to the carpenter's; so his father took him along with him.

The carpenter lived in a village, which was about a mile from Frank's home; and the way to it was by the turnpike road.

As he walked along with his father, he saw some men, who were lifting up a tree, which they had just cut down— It had been growing in a hedge by the road side—The men put the tree upon a sort of carriage; and then they dragged the carriage along the road.

" What are they going to do with this tree, papa ?" said Frank: " Will you ask them ?"

The men said, that they were carrying the tree to the saw-pit, to have it cut into boards.

They went on a little farther; and then the men turned up a lane, and dragged the carriage, with the tree upon it, after them; and Frank told his father, that he should like very much to see the saw-pit.

It was not far off; and his father went down the lane, and showed it to him.

At the saw-pit, Frank observed how the sawyer sawed wood: he looked at some boards which had just been sawed, asunder—When the sawyer rested himself, Frank looked at the large sharp teeth of his saw; and when the sawyer went on with his work, Frank's father asked him to saw slowly; and Frank observed, that the teeth of the saw cut and broke off very small parts of the wood, as the saw was pushed and drawn backwards and forwards—He saw a great deal of yellow dust in the saw-pit, which his father told him was called saw-dust; and fresh saw-dust fell from the teeth of the saw as it was moved.

The men, who had brought the tree to be sawed into boards, were all this time busy in cutting off, with a hatchet, the small branches, and Frank turned to look at what they were doing; but his father said, " Frank, I cannot wait any longer now : I have business to do at the carpenter's."—So Frank followed his father directly ; and they went on to the carpenter's.

When they came to the door of his work-shop, they heard the noise of hammering ; and Frank clapped his

hands, and said, " I am glad to hear
hammering — I shall like to hammer
myself."

" But," said his father, stopping him,
just as he pulled up the latch of the
door — " Remember that the hammer
in this house is not yours; and you
must not meddle with it, nor with any
of the carpenter's tools, without his
leave."

" Yes, papa," said Frank, " I know,
that I must not meddle with things that
are not mine — I did not meddle with
any of the flowers, or cherries, in the
gardener's nice garden; and I will not
meddle with any of the carpenter's
tools."—So his father took him into the
work-shop ; and he saw the bench
upon which the carpenter worked,
which was called a work-bench : upon
it he saw several tools, a plane, and

chisel, and a saw, and a gimlet, and a hammer : he did not meddle with any of them ; and, after his father had been some time in the work-shop, and when he saw that Frank did not touch any of these things, he asked the carpenter to let him touch them, and to show him their use.

The carpenter, who had observed that Frank had not meddled with any of his tools, readily lent them to him to look at ; and when he had looked at them, showed him their use — He planed a little slip of wood with a plane ; and he bored a hole through it with the gimlet ; and he sloped off the end of it with his chisel ; and then he nailed it to another piece of wood with nails, which he struck into the wood with his hammer.

And Frank asked if he might take

the hammer and a nail, and hammer it into a bit of wood himself.

" You may try, if the carpenter will give you leave," said his father.

So Frank took the hammer, and tried to hammer a nail into a bit of wood — He hit his fingers, instead of the nail, two or three times; but at last he drove it into the wood; and he said, " I thought it was much easier to do this, when I saw the carpenter hammering."

Frank afterwards tried to use the plane, and the saw, which he thought he could manage very easily; but he found that he could not: and he asked his father, what was the reason that he could not do all this as well as the carpenter.

The carpenter smiled, and said, " I have been learning to do all this, master; a great long while—When I first took a plane in my hand, I could not use it better than you do now."

" Then perhaps, papa, I may learn too, in time—But, papa," said Frank, recollecting his kite, " will you be so good as to ask for the slips of wood for my kite ?"

His father did so; and the carpenter found two slips that were just fit for his purpose, and gave them to him ; and his father then desired him not to talk any more ; " For," said he, " we have business to do; and you must not interrupt us."

WHILST his father was speaking to the carpenter about his own business, Frank went to the window to look at it; for it was a different sort of window

from those which he had been used to
see in his father's house—It opened
like a door; and the panes of glass
were very small, and had flat slips of
lead all round them.

Whilst Frank was examining this
window, he heard the sound of a horse
trotting; and he looked out, and he
saw a horse upon the road, which was
before the window.

The horse had a saddle and bridle
on; but nobody was riding upon it;—
It stopped and ate some grass by the
road side, and then went down a lane.

Soon after Frank had seen the horse
go by, his father, who had finished his
business with the carpenter, called to
Frank, and told him that he was going
home.

Frank thanked the carpenter for letting him look at the plane, and the saw,

and the chisel, and for giving him a slip of wood for his kite; and he took the bit of wood with him, and followed his father. When his father and he had walked a few yards from the carpenter's door, a man passed by them, who seemed very hot, and very much tired— He looked back at Frank's father, and said, "Pray, sir, did you see a horse go by this way, a little while ago?"

"No, sir, I did not," said Frank's father.

"But I did, papa," said Frank; "I saw a horse going by, upon this road, whilst I was standing, just now, at the carpenter's window."

"Pray, master, what colour was the horse you saw?" said the man.

"Black, sir," said Frank.

"Had he a saddle and bridle on?" said the man.

F 3

" Yes, sir, he had," answered Frank,

" And pray, master," said the man, " will you be so good as to tell me whether he went on, upon this road straight before us, or whether he turned down this lane to the right, or this other lane to the left hand ?"

As the man spoke, he pointed to the lanes ; and Frank answered, " The horse that I saw, sir, gallopped down this lane, to my right hand side."

" Thank you, master," said the man —" I will go after him — I hope the people at the house, yonder, will stop him.   He is as quiet and good a horse as can be, only that whenever I leave him by the road side, without tying him fast by the bridle, he is apt to stray away; and that is what he has done now."

The man, after saying this, went

down the lane to his right hand side; and Frank walked on with his father.

The road towards home was up a steep hill; and Frank began to be tired before he had got half way up the hill.

" It did not tire me so much, papa, as we came down the hill; but it is very difficult to get up it again."

" I do not hear all that you are saying," said his father, " you are so far behind me—Cannot you keep up with me ?"

" No, papa," cried Frank, as loud as he could, " because I am tired—My knees are very much tired coming up this great hill."

His father stopped, and looked back, and saw that Frank was trying to come up the hill as fast as he could.

At this time, Frank heard the noise of a horse behind him; and he looked and saw the man whom he had spoken to, a little while before, riding upon the black horse which he had seen going down the lane.

The man said to him, " Thank you, master, for telling me which way my horse went — You see I have got him again — You seem sadly tired — I will carry you up this hill upon my horse, if you have a mind."

" I will ask my father, if he likes it," said Frank.

His father said, " Yes, if you please;" and the man took Frank up, and set him before him upon the horse, and put his arm round Frank's body, to hold him fast upon the horse. Then the horse walked gently up the hill; and Frank's father walked beside him—And when they came to the top of the steep hill, his father took Frank down from the horse; and Frank thanked the man for carrying him; and he felt rested, and able to walk on merrily with his father,

And as they walked on, he said to his father, " I am glad that I saw the horse, and observed which way it went, and that I told the man which road it went. You know, papa, there were three roads; and the man could not know which way the horse went, till I told him. If I had not observed, and if I had not told him the right road, he would have gone on — on — on — on — a great way; and he would have tired himself; and he would not have found his horse."

" Very true," said his father : " now you have found one of the uses of observing what you see, and of relating facts exactly."

" *One* of the uses, papa !—Are there more uses, papa?"

" Yes, a great many."

" Will you tell them all to me?"

" I would rather that you should find them out for yourself," said his father—" You will find them all out some time or other."

Then Frank began to talk about his kite; and, as soon as he got home, his father showed him how to make it, and helped him to do it. And when it was made, he left it to dry : for the paste, which pasted the paper together, was wet; and his father told him, that it must dry before the paste would hold the paper together, and before the kite was fit to be used.

And when it was quite dry, his father told him that he might go out upon the grass, in a field near the house, and fly it.

Frank did so; and it went up very high in the air; and it staid up, now higher, now lower, for some time; and the sun shone upon it, so that it was plainly seen; and the wind swelled out the sides of it, as Frank pulled it by the middle with the string.

His mother came to the window, to look at the kite; and Frank was very glad that she saw it too, and when it came down, it fell upon the smooth grass, and it was not torn.

Frank carried it into the house, and put it by carefully, that it might not be spoiled, and that he might have the pleasure of flying it another day; and he said, " I wish I could find out why the kite goes up in the air!"

IT was a rainy day, and Frank could not go out to fly his kite—He amused himself with playing with his horse-chesnuts—He was playing in a room by himself; and, by accident, he threw one of his horse-chesnuts against the window; and it broke a pane of glass—Immediately he ran down stairs, into the room where he knew that his mother was; and he went up to her—She was speaking to somebody, and did not see him; and he laid his hand upon her arm, to make her attend to him; and the moment she turned her face to him, he said, "Mamma, I have broken the window in your bed-chamber, by throwing a horse-chesnut against it."

His mother said, " I am sorry you have broken my window; but I am glad, my dear Frank, that you come directly to tell me of it."—And his mother kissed him.

"But how shall I prevent you," said she, "from breaking my window again with your horse-chesnut?"

"I will take care not to break it again, mamma," said Frank.

"But you said that you would take care, before you broke it, to-day; and yet you see that you have broken it. After you burnt your finger by letting the hot sealing wax drop upon it you took a great deal of care not to do the same thing again, did not you?"

"Oh yes, mamma," said Frank, squeezing the finger which he burnt, just as he did at the time he burnt it—"Oh, yes, mamma, I took a great deal of care not to do the same thing again, for fear of burning myself again."

"And if you had felt some pain when

you broke the window, just now, do you not think that you should take care not to do so again?"

" Yes, mamma."

" Where is the horse-chesnut with which you broke the window?"

" It is lying upon the floor, in your room."

" Go, and fetch it."

Frank went for it, and brought it to his mother, and she took it in her hand, and said, " You would be sorry to see this horse-chesnut thrown away, would not you?"

" Yes, mamma," said Frank; " for I like to roll it about, and to play with it; and it is the only one of my horse-chesnuts that I have left."

" But," said his mother, " I am afraid that you will break another of my windows with it; and if you would throw

it away, you could not break them
with it; and the pain you would feel at
your horse-chesnut's being thrown
away, would make you remember, I
think, not to throw hard things against
glass windows again."

Frank stood for a little while, looking
at his horse-chesnut; and then he said,
"Well, mamma, I will throw it away;"
and he threw it out of the window.

Some days afterwards, his mother
called Frank to the table where she was
at work; and she took out of her work-
basket two leather balls, and gave them
to Frank; one of them was very hard,
and the other was very soft.

His mother desired, that he would
play with the soft ball when he was in
the house, and with the hard ball when
he was out of doors—She said that she
had made the soft ball on purpose for

him, that he might have one to play with when it was rainy weather, and when he could not go out.

This soft ball was stuffed with horse hair; it was not stuffed tight; and Frank could squeeze it together with his fingers.

Frank thanked his mother; and he liked the two balls very much : and his mother said to him, " You have not broken any more windows, Frank, since you *punished* yourself by throwing away your horse-chesnut; and now I am glad to *reward* you for your truth and good sense."

ABOUT a week after Frank's mother had given him the two balls, she came into the room where he had been playing at ball—Nobody had been in the room

with him, till his mother came in—She
had a large nosegay, of pinks and carnations, in her hand——" Look here,
Frank," said she : " the gardener, who
lives at the garden with the green gate,
has brought these pinks and carnations,
and has given them to me; he says
they are some of those which you
helped him to tie up."

" Oh, they are very pretty! they
are very sweet !" said Frank, smelling to them, as his mother held them
towards him —" May I help you,
mamma, to put them into the flower-
pot ?"

" Yes, my dear—Bring the flower-
pot to me, which stands on that little
table, and we will put these flowers
into it."

She sat down; and Frank ran to
the little table for the flower-pot.

" There is no water in it, mamma,"
said Frank.

" But we can put some in," said
his mother — " Well ! why do not you
bring it to me ?"

" Mamma," said Frank, " I am
afraid to take it up; for here is a great
large crack all down the flower-pot;
and when I touched it, just now, it
shook: it seems quite loose; and I
think it will fall to pieces, if I take it
in my hands."

His mother then came to the little
table, by which Frank was standing; and she looked at the flower-
pot, and saw, that it was cracked
through, from top to bottom; and, the
moment she took it in her hands, it
fell to pieces.

" This flower-pot was not broken
yesterday evening," said his mother;

" I remember seeing it without any crack in it, yesterday evening, when I took the dead minionette out of it."

" So do I, mamma; I was by at that time."

" I do not ask you, my dear Frank," said his mother, " whether you broke this flower-pot; I think, if you had broken it, you would come and tell me, as you did when you broke the pane of glass in this window."

" But, mamma," said Frank, eagerly looking up in his mother's face, " I did *not* break this flower-pot—I have not meddled with it—I have been playing with my soft ball, as you desired— Look, here is my soft ball," said he; " this is what I have been playing with all this morning."

" My dear Frank," said his mother, " I believe you. You told me the truth before, about the window that you broke."

Frank's father came into the room, at this moment; and Frank asked him, if he had broken or cracked the flower-pot.

He said, " No, I have not; I know nothing about it."

Frank's mother rang the bell, and, when the maid servant came up, asked the maid, whether she had cracked the flower-pot.

The maid answered, " No, madam, I did not." And, after she had given this answer, the maid left the room.

" Now, my dear Frank," said his father, " you see what an advantage it is to speak the truth; because I know that you told the truth about the window, which you broke, and about the horse, which you said you had seen going

down the lane, I cannot help believing
that you speak the truth now—I believe
that you did not break this flower-pot,
because you say that you did not."

" But, papa," said Frank, " I wish
that the person that *did* crack it, would
tell you or mamma, that they cracked
it, because then you would be quite,
quite sure that I did not do it—Do you
think the maid did it ?"

" No; I do not, because she says
she did not; and I have always found
that she tells the truth."

Frank's mother, whilst he was speaking, was looking at the broken pieces
of the flower-pot; and she observed,
that near the place where it was cracked,
one side of the flower-pot was blackened; and she rubbed the black, and it
came off easily; and she said, " This
looks as if it had been smoked."

"But smoke comes from the fire," said Frank, " and there has been no fire in this room, mamma."

"And did you never see smoke come from any thing but from the fire in the fire-place?"

"Not that I remember, mamma," said Frank—"Oh, yes; I have seen smoke, a great deal of smoke, come from the spout of the tea-kettle, and from the top of the urn."

"That is not smoke," said his father: " but I will tell you more about that another time — Cannot you recollect seeing smoke come from——"

"From what, papa?"

"Last night you saw smoke coming from——"

"Oh, now I recollect — from the candle, papa," said Frank.

"And now I recollect," said Frank's

father, " that late last night, I was sealing a letter at this little table; and I remember, that I left the green wax candle
burning very near this flower-pot, whilst
I went out of the room, to give the letter, which I had been sealing, to a man
who was waiting for it. When I came
back again, I put out the candle. I did
not observe, that the flower-pot was
smoked, or cracked; but I now think,
it is very probable, that the heat of that
candle cracked it."

" Let us look whether there is any
melted green wax," said Frank, " upon
the pieces of the flower-pot; because
wax, when it was melting, might drop
upon the flower-pot, as it did upon my
finger once."

Frank examined all the pieces of the
flower-pot, and on one bit, near the place
where it was blackened with smoke, he
found a round spot of green wax.

" Then," said his father, " I am now
pretty sure, that it was I, who was the
cause of cracking the flower-pot, by
putting the lighted candle too near it."

" I am very glad we have found out
the truth," said Frank; " and now,
papa," added he, " will you be so good
as to tell me about the smoke—No, not
the smoke; but the thing, that looks
so like smoke, which comes out of the
top of the urn, and out of the spout of
the tea-kettle ?"

" I have not time to explain it to
you now, Frank," said his father; " but
if I am not busy at tea-time, this evening, you may put me in mind of it
again." ——— And, at tea-time, his father showed him the difference between
smoke and steam *.

———

* See Harry and Lucy.

" The bread, mamma, is very good this morning," said Frank, one morning at breakfast.

" It is new bread."

" New bread, mamma!—What is meant by *new* bread?"

" Bread that has been newly made."

" Bread is made of flour, I remember you told me, mamma; and flour comes from —— Oh, mamma, do not you recollect telling me, that, some time or other, you would show me corn growing in the fields?—When we walk out this morning, I will put you in mind of it again."

And when he walked out with his mother in the fields, Frank put her in mind of it again; and she said, " I see some men at work, yonder, in a corn-field; let us go and see what they are

doing." So they went to the field; and
Frank's mother showed him some wheat
growing, and she showed him some that
had been cut down; she showed him
some that was ripe, and some that was
not ripe. And then they walked farther on, to the part of the field where
the men were at work.

Frank saw, that they had a kind of
sharp, bright hooks, in their hands, with
which they were cutting down the
wheat. His mother told him, that
these hooks are called reaping hooks.

He saw, that, after the wheat was cut
down, the men tied up bundles of it,
which they set upright in the field, at
regular distances from each other.
His mother told him, that each of these
bundles was called a sheaf of wheat;
and she pulled out a single stalk, and
put it into his hand, and said, "This is

called an ear of wheat — What grows upon a single stalk is called an ear of wheat."

Whilst Frank was looking at the men tying up the sheaves a person came up to him and said, " You are welcome here, master. — You are he, that was so good as to tell me, which road my horse strayed, some time ago."

Frank looked in the face of the person, who was speaking to him; and he recollected this to be the man, who carried him up the steep hill upon his horse.

This man was a farmer; and he was now overlooking some labourers, who were reaping his wheat. He pointed to a small house, amongst some trees, at a little distance; and he told Frank's mother, that he lived in that house, and that, if she would like to walk there, he

could show Frank how the men were
thrashing in his barn.

Frank's mother thanked the farmer;
and they walked to his house—It was
a thatched, white-washed house; and
it looked very neat.

There were some scarlet flowers
in the kitchen garden which looked
very pretty. As they passed through
the garden, Frank asked the name of
these flowers: and his mother told him,
that these were called scarlet runners;
and she said to him, " on this kind of
plant grow kidney beans, of which you
are so fond, Frank."

Frank saw cabbages, and cauliflowers,
and lettuce, in this garden; but his
mother said, " Come, Frank, you must
not keep us waiting;"—and he followed
his mother through a yard, where there
were a great number of ducks, and

fowls, and geese, and turkeys; and they made a great noise: and several of them clapped their white wings; and the geese and turkeys stretched out their long necks.

"You need not squeeze my hand so tight, Frank," said his mother: "You need not squeeze yourself up so close to me: these geese and turkeys will not do you any harm, though they make so much noise."

So Frank walked on stoutly; and he found that the geese and turkeys did not hurt him; and, when he had crossed this yard, the farmer led them through a gate, into a large yard, where there were ricks of hay; and there were several cows in this yard; and, as he passed by them, Frank observed that their breath smelt very sweet.

H 3

" Come this way into the barn," said the farmer: " here are the men, who are thrashing."

The barn, on the inside, looked like a large room, with rough walls and no ceiling; but it had a floor. Four men were at work in this barn: they were beating some wheat, that lay upon the floor, with long sticks; they made a great noise, as they struck the floor with their sticks, so that Frank could neither make his mother hear what he said, nor could he hear her voice.

The sticks seemed to be half broken in two, in the middle; and they seemed to swing with great violence, as the men struck with them; and Frank was afraid, that the sticks should reach to where he stood, and should hit him; but, after he had been in the barn for a little while, he became less afraid; he observed, that the sticks did not swing within reach of him.

The farmer asked the men to stop working: and they stopped; and the farmer took one of the things, with which they had been working, out of their hands, and showed it to Frank.

His mother told him, that it was called a flail. It was made of two sticks, tied together with a bit of leather.

The farmer showed Frank the wheat, which lay upon the floor; and his mother showed him, that the loose, outside cover of the wheat was beaten off by the strokes of the flail.

The farmer said, " You may take some of the wheat, master, in your hand; and some of the chaff; and then you will see the difference." The chaff, was the outside covering.

"And how is this wheat made into bread?" said Frank.

"Oh, master," said the farmer, "a great deal must be done to it before it is made into bread—It must go to the mill to be ground."

"I should like to see the mill, mamma," said Frank; "but I do not know what he means by *to be ground.*"

"That you will see, when you go to the mill."

"Shall we go to the mill now, mamma?" said Frank.

"No, my dear," said his mother; "I would rather, that you should wait till some day when your father can have time to go with you to the mill, because he can explain it to you much better than I could."

Then Frank and his mother thanked the farmer for what he had shown them; and they had a pleasant walk home.

" Ah! spare yon emmet, rich in hoarded grain;
" He lives with pleasure, and he dies with pain*."

FRANK was always careful not to hurt insects, nor any sort of animals— He liked to observe spiders in their webs, and ants carrying their white loads; but he never teized them; even those animals, which he did not think were pretty, he took care not to hurt.

One evening, when he was walking with his father and mother, upon a gravel walk near the house, he saw several black snails. He did not think them pretty animals; but, whenever he came near one, he took care not to tread upon it. He stooped down to look at one

* Sir William Jones,

of these black snails, which was drawing in its black horns———

" I believe, mamma," said Frank, " that he drew in those horns because he is afraid I am going to hurt him."

" Very likely."

" But that is foolish of the snail, mamma; because, you know, I am not going to hurt it."

" I know that, Frank; but how should the snail know it."

" He lies quite still—He will not put out his black horns again—I will go away and leave him, that I may not frighten him any more. I should not like to be frightened myself, if I was a snail," said Frank. So he ran on, before his father and mother, and left the snail ; and he saw some pretty brown and green moss upon a bank; and he asked his mother if he might gather some of it.

She said, " Yes;" and he climbed up
the bank; and he gathered some of the
moss; and, in the moss, at the foot of a
tree, he found a pretty shell: it was
striped with purple, and green, and
straw colour, and white; and it was
smooth and very shining. He got
down from the bank, as fast as he
could; and he ran and asked his mother if he might keep this pretty shell
and carry it into the house, when he
came home from walking.

His mother looked at the shell, as
Frank held it upon the palm of his hand;
and she told him, that he might have it,
and that he might carry it into the house
with him, when he went home; and
she told him that it was a snail-shell.

" A snail-shell, mamma!" said Frank;
" I never saw such a pretty snail-

shell before: I am glad I have found it; and I will take care not to break it."

Frank held it carefully in his hand, during the rest of his walk; and he often looked at it to see that it was safe; and, just as he came near the hall-door, he opened his hand and began to count the number of coloured rings upon his snail-shell—"One, two, three, four, five, rings, mamma," said Frank; "and the rings seem to wind round and round the shell; they are larger at the bottom; and they grow less, and less, and less, as they wind up to the top."

"That is called a spiral line," said his father, pointing to the line, which, as Frank said, seemed to wind round and round the shell.

As Frank was looking with attention at the shell, he felt something cold,

clammy, and disagreeable, touching his
hand, at the bottom of the shell; and
with his other hand he was going to lift
up the shell, to see what this was; but,
when he touched it, he found that it
stuck to his hand: and, a few instants
afterwards, he saw the snail-shell seemed to rise up; and he perceived the
horns and head of a snail peeping out
from beneath the shell — " Oh, mamma! there is a living snail in this shell
— Look at it," said Frank — " Look!
it has crawled out a great deal farther
now; and it carries its shell upon its
back: it is very curious; but I wish it
was crawling any where but upon my
hand; for I do not like the cold, sticky
feeling of it."

Frank then was going to shake the
snail from his hand; but he recollected
that, if he let it fall suddenly upon the

stone steps, he might hurt the animal, or break the pretty shell; therefore, he did not shake it off; but he put his hand down gently to the stone step; and the snail crawled off his hand upon the stone.

"Mamma," said Frank, "I think the snail might do without that pretty shell — You gave the shell to me, mamma — May I pull it off the snail's back?"

"My dear," said his mother, "I did not know that there was a snail in that shell, when I said that you might have it — I would not have given it to you, if I had known that there was a snail withinside of it — You cannot pull the shell from the snail's back, without hurting the animal, or breaking the shell."

"I do not wish to hurt the animal,"

said Frank; "and I am sure I do not wish to break the pretty shell, so I will not pull it—But, mamma, I think I had better take the snail and snail-shell, both together, into the house, and keep them in my little red box, mamma; what do you think?"

" I think, my dear, that the snail would not be so happy in your little red box, as it would be in the open air, upon the grass, or upon the leaves, which it usually eats."

" But, mamma, I would give it leaves to eat, in the little red box."

" But, Frank, you do not know what leaves it likes best to eat; and, if you do not shut it up in your red box, it will find the leaves for itself, which it loves best."

" Then, if you do not think it would be happy in my red box, mamma, I will not shut it up in it — I will leave it to go where it pleases with its own pretty shell upon its back — That is what I should like, if I was a snail, I believe."

He then took the snail, and put it upon the grass, and left it; and he went into the house with his mother, and she called him into her room; and she took out of her bureau something, which she held to Frank's ear; and he heard a noise like the sound of water boiling; then she put into Frank's hand what she had held to his ear; and he saw that it was a large shell, speckled red, and brown, and white; it was so large, that his little fingers could hardly grasp it.

" Do you like it as well as you did the snail-shell ?"

"Oh yes, a great deal better, mamma."

" Then I give it to you, my dear," said his mother.

" Keep it," said his father; " and, even if you keep it till you are as old as I am, you will feel pleasure, when you look at it; for you will recollect, that your mother was pleased with you, when she gave it to you, because you had been good-natured to a poor little snail."

————

" WHAT was it, mamma," said Frank, " that papa was saying to you just after you were looking at the snail?"

" I do not recollect, my dear."

" I wish you could be so good as to try to recollect, mamma; because it sounded very pretty; and I should like to hear it again—It seemed like some-

I 3

think out of a book; it was something about horned snails, and varnished shells, and sliding ——"

" Do you mean,

" Slide here, ye horned snails with varnish'd shells ? "

" Oh, yes, mamma," cried Frank, " that is what I mean; but papa said a great deal more of it—Will you say it for me ?"

" I will repeat the lines, that you may hear the agreeable sound; but I do not think that you can understand the sense of them yet," said his mother; and she repeated to him the following lines :—

" Stay thy soft-murmuring waters, gentle rill;
" Hush, whispering winds; ye rustling leaves, be still;
" Rest, silver butterflies, your quiv'ring wings;
" Alight, ye beetles, from your airy rings;
" Ye painted moths, your gold-eyed plumage furl,

" Bow your wide horns, your spiral trunks uncurl;

" Glitter, ye glow-worms, on your mossy beds;

" Descend, ye spiders, on your lengthen'd
 threads;

" Slide here, ye horned snails with varnish'd
 shells;

" Ye bee nymphs, listen in your waxen cells *."

" I do not understand the last line,
mamma, at all; but I understand about
the spiders coming down on their long
threads—I have often looked at spiders
doing that—But, mamma, I never saw
any moths, that had trunks; I do not
think, that a moth could carry a trunk."

" What do you think is meant by a
trunk, my dear?"

" A sort of box."

" That is one meaning of the word
trunk—Do you know any other meaning?"

   * Darwin.

" Yes; trunk of a tree."

" And did you never see the picture of the trunk of an elephant ? "

" Yes, yes, mamma; I remember seeing that, and I remember you read to me an account of the elephant; and you told me, that he could curl up that trunk of his—But, mamma, such moths as I have seen are little flying animals, about as large as a butterfly: they could not have such trunks as elephants have."

" No, they have not: they have not such large trunks."

" Will you tell me what sort of trunks they have ? "

" I will show you, the first time we see a moth."

" Thank you, mamma: and I wish you could show me a glow worm—I have seen a beetle—But, mamma, will

ıu say that part about the beetle
ʒain ?"

" Alight, ye beetles, from your airy rings."

" What does that mean, mamma ?"

" Beetles sometimes fly round and
ɔund, in the air, so as to make the
shape of circles or rings in the air; and
alight, here, means come down from
——alight upon the ground, or settle
upon the ground."

" And *silver butterflies*, mamma,
does not mean, made of silver, but
that they look shining, like silver; does
not it ?"

" Yes, my dear."

" But I wish, very much, mamma, to
see the glow-worms, that lie on the
mossy beds."

" I will try if I can find a glow-worm,
and show it to you, this evening," said
his mother.

In the evening, when it was dusk,
Frank's mother called him, and bid him
follow her; and she went down a lane,
that was near her house; and Frank
followed her—She looked from side to
side, on the banks, and under the
hedges, as she walked along.

" Are you looking for a glow-worm,
mamma?" said Frank; " it is so dark
now, that I am afraid we shall not see
it, unless it is a great deal larger than
a common worm, or unless we had a
lanthern—May I go back for the little
lanthern, that is in the hall; there is a
candle ready lighted in it, mamma—
May I go back for it, mamma?"

" No, my dear; we shall not want
a lanthern, nor a candle—We shall be
more likely to find a glow-worm in the
dark, than if we had a candle."

Frank was surprised at hearing his

mother say this—" I can always find
things better in the light than in the
dark," said he——But, just as he
finished speaking, he saw a light upon
the bank, near the place where his mother was standing; and she called to
him, and said, " Here is a glow-worm,
Frank; come nearer to me, and you
will see it better."

Frank kneeled down upon the bank,
beside his mother, and he saw, that the
light seemed to come from the tail of
a little brown caterpillar.

The caterpillar crawled on, upon the
bank; and the light moved on, whenever the caterpillar moved, and stood
still, whenever it stood still.

Frank's mother, whilst the glow-
worm was standing still, put her hand
down upon the bank, close beside it;

and, by-and-by, the glow-worm began to move again; and it crawled upon her hand.

"Oh, mamma! take care," cried Frank, "it will burn you."

"No, my dear, it will not burn me, it will not hurt me," said his mother; and she held her hand towards Frank; and he saw the glow-worm upon it.

"Shall I put it in your hand?" said his mother.

Frank drew back, as if he was still a little afraid that it should burn him.

"My dear," said his mother, "it will not hurt you—You know, that I would not tell you that it would not hurt you, if it would—You know, that I told you the hot melting sealing-wax would scald you, if you let it drop upon your fingers, and it did—But I tell you, that the light, which you see about this animal, will not burn you, as the flame of a candle, or as the fire would."

" Then, here is my hand, mamma— Put the glow-worm upon it; and I will not shrink back again," said Frank.

He found, that the light from the glow-worm did not hurt him in the least; and he asked his mother how it came, that this, which looked so much like the flame of a candle, should not burn him.

But she answered, " I cannot explain that to you, my dear."

And when Frank had looked at the glow-worm as long as he liked to do so, his mother desired him to put it again upon the bank; and he did so; and, before they got home, Frank saw several other glow-worms upon the banks,

and his mother said to him, " Now you
know the meaning of

' Glitter, ye glow-worms, on your mossy beds.'"

" Yes," said Frank, " *glitter*, means,
look bright, shine—Thank you, mamma, for showing me these glow-worms;
and, some time or other, I hope we shall
see the trunk of a moth."

————

THE candles were lighted, and all
the window-shutters in the room were
shut, except the shutters of one window,
which were left open to let in air; for
it was a warm evening.

Frank's mother was sitting upon a
sofa, reading; and Frank was kneeling
upon a chair at the table upon which
the candle stood. He was looking at

some prints, in a book, which his mother had lent to him.

Through the window which was open,
there flew into the room a large moth—
It flew towards the candle.

"Oh, mamma! here is a moth,"
cried Frank.

As he spoke, the moth, which had
flown very quickly round and round the
candle, two or three times, went so close
to the flame, that Frank thought it
would burn itself to death; and he
cried, "Oh, it will burn itself!" and
he put his hand before his eyes, that he
might not see the moth burn itself——
But his mother did not put her hand
before her eyes: she got up as quickly
as possible, and put her hand gently
over the moth, and caught it; and so
prevented it from burning itself in the
candle.

"I am glad you have caught it, mamma," said Frank; "and the next time, I will try to catch it as you did; and I will not put my hands before my eyes, because that did the moth no good."

His mother then covered the moth with a glass tumbler; and she put it upon the table; and Frank looked through the glass; and he saw it plainly.

When the moth was quiet, Frank's mother took a honey-suckle out of her nosegay; and she lifted up one side of the tumbler, a little way from the table; and she squeezed the honey-suckle under the tumbler; and as soon as the moth perceived the flower was near him, he walked upon it, and Frank saw him uncurl what is called his trunk, or proboscis; and he saw the moth dip it into

part of the flower of the honey-suckle
—And he saw also what were called
the horns of the moth; and he saw the
animal bow them forwards; and he said,
" Now, mamma, will you repeat those
two lines about the moth again, for
me ?"

" Ye painted moths, your gold-eyed plumage
    furl;
" Bow your wide horns, your spiral trunks un-
    curl."

" *Painted !*" said Frank—" it does
not mean that the moth is painted, I
suppose, but that it looks as if it was
painted—*Gold-eyed plumage*, mamma !
What does that mean ?"

" *Plumage* means feathers, such as
you see on birds—Look through this
glass," said his mother, putting a magnifying-glass into his hand.

" I have looked through this glass

before at a caterpillar, mamma: it
makes things look larger."

His mother lifted up the tumbler
gently; and, as the moth was settled
upon the honey-suckle, Frank looked
through the magnifying-glass at it.

" Mamma, it looks very large ; and
upon its wings," said Frank, " I see
what look like very, very small feathers."

" That is what is meant by *plumage*."

" But *gold-eyed*, mamma!—I see no
gold eyes."

" Do you see some spots upon the
wings?"

" Dark brown spots, mamma?"

" Yes."

" They are of the shape of eyes; and
though they are not eyes, they are called
so, from their shape.   In some moths,

those spots are yellow, gold-coloured; and then they may be called *gold-eyed.*"

"One thing more, mamma," said Frank: "What does it mean by——Would you be so good as to say the last line again; for I do not recollect the word that I did not understand."

His mother repeated the line again—

"Ye painted moths, your gold-eyed plumage furl."

"*Furl,* mamma—Furl is the word which I do not understand."

His mother showed him a fan, and showed him what is meant by *to furl* and *unfurl* a fan; and when the moth closed and afterwards spread its wings, she said, "now he is furling, and now he is unfurling, his pretty wings: *furl* and *unfurl* are seaman's phrases, and are used *metaphorically,* in speaking of a fan, or of a moth's wings."

" Metaphorically! mamma," said Frank, " I think that is a harder word than furl."

" It is, my dear," said his mother; " but I will explain it to you. When a word, that properly belongs to one kind of thing, is made use of in speaking of another kind of thing, then it is used *metaphorically*. As the word *furl*, which is properly used in speaking of the sails of a ship, and metaphorically in speaking of a moth's wings—But now I think we have kept the poor moth long enough under this glass—We will now let him fly about where he pleases."—So she took the moth, and let him fly out of the window.

"Do you know, mamma," said Frank, " that I can repeat those two lines about the moths;—I wish you would say the other lines again for me, that I might learn them all, and then say them to my father; I think he would like to hear me say them after dinner, to morrow, mamma?"

" I think your father will like to hear you repeat them, if you understand them all, but not otherwise."

" I think I do understand them all— every one now, mamma, except something in the last line, about bees in their waxen cells."

" You never saw a honey-comb: did you, Frank?"

" No, mamma, never."

" When you see a honey-comb, you will know what is meant by the waxen cells in which bees live."

THE next morning at breakfast, there was part of a honey-comb upon a plate, on the breakfast-table; and Frank's mo-

ther showed it to him; and she gave
him some honey.—He liked the sweet
taste of the honey: and he thought the
honey-comb was very pretty. His mother
gave him a little bit of the honey-comb,
which she told him was made of wax.

"It is quite a different sort of
wax from sealing-wax, mamma," said
Frank: "where does this wax come
from, and this pretty honey-comb, and
this sweet honey?"

His mother told him, that she would
show him where they all came from,
when she had finished eating her breakfast—And, after breakfast was over,
she took Frank with her to a cottage,
belonging to an old woman in the
neighbourhood.

The old woman was sitting at her
door turning a small wheel very quickly round, which Frank's mother told him
was called a spinning-wheel.

The old woman pushed her spinning-wheel on one side, and got up, as soon as they came to her door.

"Thank you for the good honey you sent us, Mrs. Wheeler," said Frank's mother.

"You are heartily welcome, ma'am, I'm sure," said the old woman; "but it was not *I* that sent it; it was my grandson sent it to you——George! George! are you there?"

A little boy came running to the door; and he smiled when he saw Frank; and Frank smiled when he saw him; for he recollected that this was the same boy to whom he had returned the nuts, which he had found dropped near the stile—the same boy, who had brought him back his ripe bunch of cherries.

"Thank you for the honey you sent us," said Frank's mother to this boy;

" will you be so good as to let us look at your bee-hive?—I hear that you have a glass bee-hive."

" Yes, ma'am, I have," said the boy; " and, if you will be pleased to come with me, into the garden, I will show it to you—I have a glass bee-hive; and I have a straw bee-hive."

Frank and his mother followed the boy, who ran across a narrow passage, which went straight through the house; and he opened a low gate, and took them into a small garden. The paths were narrow; and he said to Frank, " Take care that you do not prick yourself against the gooseberry-bushes, as I do when I am in a hurry to get by."

Frank took care not to prick himself; and the boy pointed to his bee-hives, and said, " There are my bee-hives, and there are my bees."

" Did bees make that straw basket?"
said Frank.

The boy laughed so much at this
question, that he could make no answer; but Frank's mother answered,
" No, my dear; the bees did not make
that straw basket; that was made by
men; but go and look in, through the
little pane of glass in that wooden box,
and you will see what bees make."

" Do not you know," said the little
boy, " what bees make? I thought
every body knew that bees make honey
and wax."

" How can they make honey? What
do they make it of?" said Frank.

" They collect it; they get it from
flowers," answered his mother: and
she said to the boy, " May I gather
this honey-suckle?" touching a honey-suckle, which grew in an arbour.

close beside the place where she stood.

"Yes, and welcome, ma'am," said the boy; "that honey-suckle is mine: grandmother gave it to me."

When Frank's mother had gathered the honey-suckle, she pulled off a part of the flower; and she held that end of the flower, which grew next the stalk, to Frank's mouth; and she bid him suck it.

He sucked it.

"It has a sweet taste, like honey," said Frank—"Is that the reason the flower is called honey-suckle, mamma?"

"Yes, my dear, I believe it is."

"And have all flowers honey in them, mamma?"

"I do not know, my dear; but I know, that some flowers have more ho-ney in them than others."

" And how do bees get honey from flowers?"

" Look, and you may see a bee now settling upon that honey-suckle in the arbour: you will see all that I have seen, if you use your own little eyes."

Frank used his own little eyes; and he saw, that the bee stretched out its proboscis, or trunk, and put it down into the flower, then drew it back again, and flew to another part of the flower, settled again, and again put down its proboscis, drew it back, and put it to its mouth.

" I fancy, mamma, the bee sucks the honey, which it gets in the flower, from its proboscis, every time it puts it to its mouth—But I am not sure; because I do not see the honey."

" You are very right not to say, that you are sure of it, as you do not see it;

but I believe that the bee does, as you say, draw the honey from flowers with that proboscis; and then he puts the honey into his mouth, and then swallows the honey. With a good magnifying glass, you might see that the proboscis of the bee is rough, and you might see the little drops of honey sticking to it. The bee gets but one or two very small drops of honey from one flower."

" What a great deal of work it must be, then, for the bees to collect as much honey as I ate this morning at breakfast! But, mamma, does this bee swallow all the honey it gets from this flower?"

" Yes, the bee swallows it; it keeps the honey in a little bag; and the bee has the power of forcing it up again from this bag, whenever it pleases.

Usually the bee carries the honey home
to the hive, and puts it in the little
waxen cells; such as those you saw in
the honey-comb, to day at breakfast."

" And where do the bees get the
wax, mamma, of which they make the
cells in the honey-comb?"

" I am not sure, my dear, what that
wax is—I believe, that it is made partly
of farina, which the bees collect from
the flowers, and partly of some sticky
substance in the stomachs of bees.
Some time or other, you will read the
accounts, which have been written of
bees, and then you will judge for yourself."

Frank looked through the glass pane,
into the bee-hive; but he said, that the
bees crowded so close to one another,
that he could not see what they were
doing.

His mother told him, that some other day she would bring him again to see the bees at work, and that, by degrees, perhaps he would distinguish them, and see what they were doing.

When Frank went home, he said, " Now mamma, that I know what is meant by the bees in their waxen cells, may I learn those lines, and will you repeat them to me ?"

" It is troublesome to me, my dear," said his mother, " to repeat them so often over; but here is a book in which you can read them yourself; and you may now learn them by rote, if you like it."

FRANK read the lines over and over, and tried to learn them by rote; and at last he could repeat them, as he thought, perfectly ; and one day, after dinner, he went to his father, and told him, that he could repeat some pretty lines to him, if he would give him leave.

"I shall be glad to hear them, Frank," said his father, " begin and repeat them." So Frank repeated them, without making any mistakes; and, when he had repeated them, his father asked him several questions about them, to try whether he understood them ; and his father was pleased to find that he really did understand; and Frank told him; that his mother had been so good as to show him a glow-worm, and a moth; and a bee-hive, and that she had explained to him all the words in the lines, which he did not at first understand.

" I am glad, my dear," said his father, " that you have had so much amusement, and that you have had the perseverance to learn any thing well, that you began to learn—But, pray, tell me why you have been continually buttoning and unbuttoning the left sleeve of your coat, whilst you have been talking to me, and whilst you were repeating these verses?"

" I do not know, papa," said Frank, laughing, "only I remember, that, when I was getting the verses by rote, and saying them by myself, I first began buttoning and unbuttoning this sleeve, and then I could not say the verses so well without doing that."

" And do not you remember, Frank," said his mother, " that I spoke to you, several times, and told you, that I was afraid you would get a trick, a habit of buttoning and unbuttoning that sleeve of yours, if you did not take care?"

" Yes, mamma, said Frank; " and

I stopped whenever you spoke to me, and whenever I remembered it; but then I found myself doing it again, without thinking of it; and now, whenever I am trying to recollect any thing, I cannot recollect it half so well without buttoning and unbuttoning my sleeve."

" Give me your right hand," said his father.

Frank gave his hand to his father.

" Now," said his father, " repeat those lines to me once more."

Frank began—

" Stay thy soft-murmuring waters, gentle rill;
" Hush, whispering winds——"

But here he twitched his hand, which his father held fast—

" Hush, whispering winds——

" Father, I cannot say it whilst you hold my hand."

His father let go his hand.

Frank immediately buttoned and un-
buttoned his sleeve, and then repeated,
very fluently—

"Hush, whispering winds; ye rustling leaves,
   be still;
" Rest, silver butterflies——

But here his father caught hold of his
right hand; and he could get no farther.

" My dear," said his father, " it would
be very inconvenient to you, if your
memory was to depend upon your button; for you see, that I can make you
forget all you have to say in an instant,
by only catching hold of your hand."

" But then, papa, if you would be so
good as not to catch hold of my hand,"
said Frank, " you would hear how well
I could repeat the lines."

" It is of little consequence," said his
father, " whether you repeat these lines

to-day, or to-morrow; but it is of great consequence, that you should not learn foolish, awkward tricks: therefore, I beg you will not say them to me again, till you can hold yourself perfectly still whilst you are repeating them."

———

FRANK'S father and mother went out to walk, and Frank went with them. ——"Oh, I am glad you are going this way," said Frank, "because now I shall see the swing."

His father had had a swing put up between two trees. Frank had seen it, from the window of the room in which he slept; but he had never yet been close to it; and he wished very much to see it, and to swing in it.

When he came up to it, he found that there was a soft cushion, fastened to the middle of the rope of which the swing was made.

One end of the rope was tied round the trunk of a large ash tree, and the other end of the rope was tied round the trunk of an oak, that was opposite to the ash.

The rope was tied towards the top of the trees; and some of the branches of the trees were cut away, so that the rope could swing backwards and forwards, without catching in any thing.

The cushion, which made the seat of the swing, hung so near the ground, that Frank could reach it; and he asked his father, whether he might sit upon it.

His father told him, that he might; and he said, " Take hold of the cord on each side of you, and hold it fast, and your mother and I will swing you."

Frank jumped up on the cushion directly, and seated himself, and took hold of the cord, on each side of him, with each of his hands.

" You must take care not to let go the cord whilst we are swinging you," said his father, " or perhaps you will tumble out of the swing, and be hurt —hold up your feet, that they may not touch the ground."

" I will not let go, papa: I will hold fast," said Frank: and his father and mother began to swing him backwards and forwards; he liked it very much; but it was a sharp evening in autumn, and his father and mother did not like to stand still long, to swing him.

" When you have had twenty more swings backwards and forwards, we will stop, Frank," said his father—So Frank began to count the swings; and

whilst he was counting, a leaf fell from
the tree, and put him out; and he tried
to recollect whether the last number of
swings he had counted to himself, was
six or seven: and the moment he began to try to recollect this, he let go the
cord with his right hand; for he was
going to button and unbutton his sleeve,
as he had the habit of doing, when he
was trying to recollect any thing.

The moment he let go the cord, he
twisted a little in the seat, and could
not catch the cord again; and he fell
out of the swing.

He fell on the grass, and he hurt his
ancle, but not much.

" It is well you were not more hurt,"
said his father—" If we had been
swinging you higher, and if you had
fallen upon the gravel-walk, instead of
on the grass, you might have been very

much hurt——My dear, why did you let go the cord?"

"Papa," said Frank, "because I was trying to recollect whether it was six swings or seven, that I had had."

"Well, and could not you recollect that without letting go the cord?"

"No, papa—the thing was—that I was, I believe, going to button my sleeve—I wish I had not that trick."

"You may cure yourself of it, if you take pains to do so," said his father.

"I wish I could," said Frank: "my uncle is not very much hurt, however. —Papa, will you put me into the swing again, and I think I shall take more care not to let go the cord now—You know I have not had all my twenty swings, papa."

"No; you have had but eight," said his father; "but I am afraid, that, if

I were to put you into the swing again, and if you were to begin counting again, if you should not be able to recollect the number, you would let go the cord to button your sleeve, and you would slip out of the swing again."

"No, papa," said Frank, " I think this is the very thing, that would cure me of that trick, because that I do not like to tumble down and hurt myself; and I think I should take care, and count, and recollect, without buttoning or unbuttoning this sleeve—May I try, papa?"

His father shook hands with him, and said, " I am glad to see, that you can bear a little pain, and that you wish to cure yourself of this foolish trick—Jump, my boy," said his father; and Frank sprung up, and his father seated him in the swing again.

He counted, and held fast by the rope, this time; and just when he was come to the eighteenth swing, his father said to him, " Can you recollect the last number you counted, without letting go the rope to button your sleeve?"

"Yes, papa," said Frank, "I can: it was seventeen."

"And you have had two swings since I spoke last; how many does that make?"

Frank was just going to let go the cord, to button his sleeve; but he recollected his former tumble — He held fast; and, after thinking for an instant, answered, " Seventeen swings and two swings make nineteen swings."

His father then gave him one good swing more, and then lifted him out; and his mother kissed him.

The next day, his father was going

from home; and, when he took leave of Frank, Frank asked him, if there was any thing he could do for him whilst he was away—" May I dust the books in your study, papa? I can do that," said Frank.

" I would rather, my dear," said his father, " that you should, whilst I am away, learn to repeat the lines, which you got by heart, without——"

" I know what you mean, papa; I will try if I can."

His father went away; and Frank, after he was gone, asked his mother, if she would take him to the swing, and swing him, and let him try whether he could recollect some of the verses whilst he was swinging; " for then, you know, mamma, I cannot move my hands without tumbling out; and I shall take care."

But his mother said, that she did not choose to swing him, whilst his father was away; and Frank, soon afterwards, said, " will you be so good, then, mamma, as to cut off this button, and to sew up this button-hole for me, and then I cannot button and unbutton it."

His mother cut off the button, and sewed up the button-hole; and several times, when he was trying to repeat the lines, he felt for the button and button-hole; but, when he found that the button was gone, and that he could not put his finger into the button-hole, he, by degrees, left off feeling for them.

His father staid away a week; and, in this time, Frank quite cured himself of the foolish trick, which he had had, and he repeated the lines to himself, whilst he held his hands quite still.

He asked his mother to sew on the

button again, and to open the button-hole, the day his father came home; and she did so.

And when his father came home, and after he had said, " How do you do, father?" Frank cried, " May I say the lines now, father?"

" Yes, my dear."

He stood opposite to his father, held his hands perfectly still, and repeated the lines without making a single mistake.

His father was pleased; and he desired the servant, who was bringing some things of his out of the chaise, in which he came, to give him a book, that was in the front pocket of the chaise.

The book was Bewick's History of Quadrupeds: it had very pretty prints in it.—Frank's father wrote in a blank page at the beginning of it—

" This book was given to Frank, October the 27th, 1798, by his father, as a mark of his father's approbation for his having, at six years old, cured himself of a foolish habit."

" Read that if you can, Frank," said his father.

Frank could not read all the words; for he was not used to read writing; but his mother read it to him.

And Frank liked the prints in this book very much, and he said, " Shall I read all that is in the book, papa ?"

" Read only what you can understand, and what entertains you in it, my dear," said his father.

FRANK was kneeling upon a chair, beside the table upon which his mother was writing. He was looking at the prints in his Bewick, and every minute he exclaimed, "Oh, mamma, look at this!—Mamma, here is a very pretty print! Only look at this one, mamma—the old, old man, going over a narrow bridge, and his dog leading him—He is a blind man, I suppose; and the wind has blown his hat off; and it is raining very hard—Pray look, mamma!"

His mother put down her pen; and she looked at the print, which she said was very pretty.

"But now, Frank," added she, "do not interrupt me any more."

Frank was silent after this; but, whenever he turned over a new leaf, he put down both his elbows upon the table, to look at the new print; and he shook the table, so that his mother could not write; wherefore she at last de-

sired him to take his book to another
table.

He did so; but he said, that he could
not see nearly so well as when he was
nearer to the light.

"If you had not disturbed me," said
his mother, "I should not have sent
you away from this table. You should
consider what is agreeable to others, or
they will not consider what is agreeable
to you."

"Mamma," said Frank, "if you will
let me come back to the table where
you are sitting, I will take care not to
shake the table."

His mother told Frank, that he might
come; and he took care not to shake
the table.

A little while after this, he was trying
to draw the old man, going over the
bridge. Pompey, a little dog, that was

in the room, jumped up, suddenly,
behind Frank's chair, and shook the
table.

"Fie! Pompey! fie!—down! down!"
cried Frank—"I don't like you, Pompey, at all."

"Why don't you like Pompey?"
said Frank's mother—"you generally
are very fond of him."

"Yes, mamma, so I am fond of him,
generally; but I don't like him now,
because he shook me, and hindered me
drawing——Oh, Pompey! Pompey!
again you gave my elbow a great shake
——Look, mamma, just as I was drawing the old man's nose, he shook me."

"Who? the old man?"

"No, mamma, but Pompey. Just
as I was drawing the old man's nose,
Pompey shook me, and made me make
the old man's nose as large as his whole

head——Oh, Pompey! you have spoiled my old man entirely—But I'll rub out his nose, and draw it over again."

Just as Frank had finished dráwing the old man's nose over again, the dog shook him again; and Frank was angry —"Don't shake, Pompey—I have bid you several times not to shake, and still you go on shaking—Naughty Pompey! Why don't you do as you are bid?"

"Perhaps the dog does not understand you," said Frank's mother.

"Well, but it is very disagreeable that he should shake the table——I don't like him at all to night."

Here Frank began struggling with Pompey. Pompey had his fore paws upon the table; and Frank was trying to drag him back by the hind legs; but all this struggling shook the table very much.

" Frank, I don't like either you, or Pompey, now," said Frank's mother, " because you both of you shake the table, so that I cannot write—Look, here is an O that is as crooked as your old man's nose."

" I am very sorry, mamma," said Frank; " but will you be so kind as to put Pompey out of the room ; and then we shall all be quiet and happy ——You know you sent me to another table when I was troublesome ; and now, if you put Pompey out of the room, he cannot be troublesome to us any more."

" Very true," said his mother ; and she put Pompey out of the room.

" I am glad he is gone," cried Frank: " now I can draw nicely."

" And now I can write nicely," said his mother.

" Mamma, are you glad when I go out of the room, after I have been troublesome, as we are now, that we have got rid of Pompey ?"

" Yes."

" But when I am not troublesome, you are not glad when I go out of the room."

" No; I am glad to have you with me, when you are not troublesome."

" And you are more glad to have me with you when I am useful to you, as I was yesterday, when I helped you to cut open the leaves of those new books, which you wanted to read — You liked me very much then, when you said I was *useful* to you."

" Yes; people like those that are useful to them."

" And I like to be liked, mamma, by you, more than by any body, so I will try always to be as useful to you as I can—I can be useful to you now, mamma, if you will give me leave."

" I will give you leave, and welcome, Frank," said his mother, smiling—So Frank went for a little bit of wood, which his father had given to him; and he cut it with his knife, into the shape of a wedge: and he put this wedge under one of the legs of the table, which was shorter than the other legs; and the table was now much steadier than it was before.

" Now, mamma," said Frank, " try to shake the table, and you will feel how steady it is—I can put my elbows upon it now, without shaking it; and, I dare say, even Pompey would not shake it, if he was to leap up as he did just now—Is not my wedge useful, mamma?"

" Yes; thank you for it, my dear."

" And now, mamma, may I open the door, and let poor Pompey in again; for he cannot easily shake us now?"

Frank's mother told him that he might let Pompey in again; and when Frank opened the door he saw Pompey, sitting upon his hind legs, holding something up in his fore paws.

" Oh, mamma, it is my glove," cried Frank; " the glove that I lost yesterday —Useful Pompey! I like you for finding my glove.—Useful Pompey!—Come in, useful Pompey!"

ONE evening, at tea-time, there was a small plum cake upon a plate, on the tea-table; and there was a knife beside the plate. Frank's father and mother, and two of his brothers, were sitting round the table; his mother was beginning to pour out the tea; and she called to Frank, and said to him, " My dear, cut this plum cake into five pieces for us; and take care, that you make all the pieces of the same size, for your father, and your two brothers, and yourself, and me; and give us each a just share."

Frank began to cut the cake; but, by mistake, he divided it into six parts, instead of into five.

- " Mamma," said he, " what shall I do with this bit? I have five without it; one for you, and one for my father, and one for my brother Edward, and one for my brother Harry, and one for myself— What shall I do with this bit that is left?"

" What is it most just to do with it ?"

" I think I had better keep it myself, mamma, because it belongs to nobody; and I should have it for the trouble of cutting the cake for every body."

" No," said his brother Henry, " I do not think *that* would be just, because, then, you would be rewarded for making a mistake ; if you had cut the cake rightly, there would not be this bit to spare."

" Well," said Frank, " I do not think it would be just, that I should have it; but who, then, shall I give it to ?—I will give it to you, mamma, because I like to give it to you best——No, I will give it to papa, because he likes plum cake better than you do——Stay, I will give it to you, good Henry, be-

cause you mended my kite for me.——
No, indeed, I must give it to poor Edward, because he had no cherry pie, to day, at dinner."

"But," said his mother, "what right have you, Frank, to give this bit of cake to poor Edward, because he had no cherry pie to day, at dinner; or to good Henry, because he mended your kite; or to your father, because he loves plum cake better than I do; or to me, because you like to give it to me?—What right have you to give it away to any of us?"

"Mamma, you said, that I was to give each of you your just share; and I thought I was to be judge."

"Remember, that I desired you to divide the cake into five pieces, all of the same size; you were to judge about the size of the pieces; and you were to take care, that we have each our just share; but you are going to give one of us twice as much as any of the others."

" I cannot make the pieces the right size, now, mamma."

" But you can give us each equal quantities of cake; cannot you ? "

" How, mamma ? "

" Think —When you are trusted to divide any thing, you must take the trouble, Mr. Judge, to consider how it is to be done fairly."

Frank took the trouble to think; and he then cut the spare bit of cake into five equal parts; and he put these parts by the side of the five large pieces of cake; and he gave one of the large pieces, and one of the little pieces, to each person; and he then said, " I believe I have divided the cake fairly now."

—Every body present said " *Yes;*" and every body looked carefully at each of the shares; and there appeared exactly the same quantity in each share—So each person took their portion; and all were satisfied—Justice satisfies every body.

" My dear Frank," said his mother, " as you have divided the cake so fairly, let us see how you will divide the sugar, that was upon the top of the cake, and which is now broken and crumbled to pieces in the plate—We all like that sugar: divide it equally amongst us."

" But this will be very difficult to do, mamma," said Frank, " because the pieces of sugar are all of such different sizes and shapes; and here are so many crums of cake mixed with the crums of sugar, I do not know how I shall ever divide it exactly—Will it do, if I do not divide quite exactly, mamma?"

"No," said his mother, "I beg you will divide it quite exactly: you can do it, if you take the right way to do it."

Frank first took out all the largest bits of sugar, and laid them upon one another, and broke off the corners and edges till he thought he made five of them of the same size exactly; and then he divided the crums, and little broken bits, into five heaps, which he thought seemed to be of the same size.

But, when he had done, his brother Henry said, "This heap next me is a great deal larger than any of the others."

And Edward said, "My heap is taller than yours; but it is not so closely squeezed together; and that makes a great difference."

And his father said, "Frank, my

large bit of sugar is twice as big as your largest bit."

" Oh, no, indeed, papa, I measured them; and they are exactly the same size: put yours upon mine, and you shall see— Look papa—not the least .corner, or crum, difference.

" They are of the same length and breadth, I acknowledge," said his father; " but they are not of the same thickness."

" Oh, thickness! I never thought of thickness."

" But you should think of it," said his father, " because— Look here— If I was to cut my bit of sugar, which is twice as thick as yours, into two slices, each of those slices would be as long, and as broad, and as thick, as your bit is now, and I should have two bits of the same size as yours—twice as much as you."

" Ah! so you would — Thickness does make a great difference—Then how shall I manage; for, if I begin to cut the sugar, in your way, in slices——Look, papa, it all crumbles—Indeed the crums are the most easily divided. I will crumble it all, and then divide the crums amongst you, and then I shall have no difficulty about the thickness."

So Frank pounded the sugar with a spoon, till it was all become a fine powder, and then he divided it into heaps; but still, people did not agree, that his heaps were all of the same size.

" We can measure them," said Frank; and he put one of the heaps into a tea-spoon; it did not quite fill the spoon—another of the heaps filled the spoon higher than the brim—Another was exactly a spoonful—Frank added to one heap, and took from another.

"You squeeze the sugar in the spoon, and that will make more go in than there should," said Henry.

"Indeed! Indeed!" said Frank, "it cannot be divided more exactly. It is impossible to divide the sugar more exactly than I have done it now; is not it, mamma?"

"I cannot say, that it is impossible to divide it more exactly," said his mother, smiling; "but, as far as I can guess, by looking at your heaps, they seem to be of the same size; I cannot, however, be sure, merely by looking at them, that they contain exactly equal quantities."

"How then could you be sure? I do not feel any difference, mamma.

Perhaps I could find out by weighing
them in a pair of scales——Papa, will
you be so good as to lend me the scales
in which you were weighing——money, I believe, yesterday?"

" No, my dear," said his father, " the
saucers of those scales are made of
brass; and you must not put any thing,
that you are going to eat, near brass,
because the rust of brass is poisonous
——I will lend you another pair of
scales, which are made of ivory; and
in these you may weigh your sugar——
Go for these scales: they are upon the
table, that is on the right hand side of
the window, in my study. As you
are used to find your way about the
house in the dark you will readily find
what you want."

Frank found the scales, and weighed
his heaps of sugar very carefully. He
was surprised to find, that there was so

much difference in the weight of the
heaps, which he thought were exactly
of the same size.   By patiently adding
and taking away, he at last, however,
made them each of the same weight,
and every body was then satisfied with
the accuracy of his division.

" Now, Frank, eat your own share of
cake, and drink his dish of tea, which
has grown quite cold, whilst you have
been dividing and weighing," said his
mother.   And, whilst Frank and his
brothers were eating their shares of
plum-cake, Frank's father said, that, if
they pleased, he would read a short
story to them.

The boys said, that they should like
to hear a story; and the story, that he
read, was out of Sandford and Merton—
Cyrus's judgment about the two coats.

ONE day, Frank went with his mother to a shop in a town: it was a shop where gloves, and ribands, and caps, and hats, were sold. His mother, after she had bought some gloves, which she wanted, went into a little room behind the shop to see a poor girl, who was ill.

"Frank," said his mother, "stay in this shop till I come back again."

Frank staid in the shop; and, whilst he was there, a carriage stopped at the door: and a lady got out of the carriage, and came into the shop where Frank was: she asked to look at some ribands; and, whilst the shopman was looking in some little drawers for ribands, the lady turned to look at Frank, and said, "Does this little boy belong to you?" meaning the shopkeeper.

O 3

" Oh, no, ma'am ; he belongs to a lady, who is just gone into the next room ;" and the shop-keeper mentioned the name of Frank's mother.

The moment the lady heard this, she smiled at Frank, called him to her, kissed him, and told him he was a charming little creature. She then asked him several questions; and Frank was pleased by her smiling at him and praising him ; and he began to talk to her; and then she said he was the finest boy she had ever seen in her life; and he liked her still better.

She was rolling up some riband in a paper, upon which some words were printed; and she asked him whether he could read any of those words. " Oh, yes," said Frank; and he read, " Sars-nets, modes, and peelings—the most fashionable assortment."

The lady stopped his mouth by kissing him; and she told him he was a very clever little fellow indeed.

Frank thought he should appear to her still cleverer, if he repeated the pretty verses, which he had learned by heart.——" Oh, what a memory he has! I never heard any thing so well repeated!" exclaimed the lady.

Frank went on to tell her the history of his having cured himself of the trick of buttoning and unbuttoning his coat; and he told her that his father had given him a book; and he repeated, word for word, what his father had written at the beginning of his book.

To all this the lady listened with a smiling countenance; and Frank was going on, talking about himself, when his mother came out of the room at the back of the shop; and she called Frank, and took him home with her.

The next day, his mother, who usually let Frank read to her a little every day, told him that he might bring his book to her and read. He began to read; and he made several mistakes; and his mother said, " Frank, you are not minding what you are about this morning."

Frank read on, more carefully: and when he had read about half a page, without making any mistake, he stopped short, and said to his mother, " But mamma, you do not praise me as the lady in the shop did."

" I do not flatter you, my dear," said his mother.

" What is flattering me, mamma!"

" Flattering you, my dear, is prais--

ing you more than you deserve to be praised."

" Did the lady in the shop flatter me, mamma ?"

" I do not know; for I was not by : I did not hear what she said."

" She said—I feel, mamma, I do not know why, ashamed to tell you all she said to me—She said, I was a charming little creature, and that I was the finest boy she had ever seen in her life; and she said, I was a very clever little boy indeed, when I read something about sarsnets and modes, that was printed on a paper, in which she was rolling up some riband; and when I repeated the verses to her, mamma, she said she never heard any thing so well repeated in her life."

" And did you believe all this, Frank ?"

"Not quite, mamma—I made some mistakes, when I was repeating the verses; and she did not take notice of that."

" And did you understand what you read about sarsnets and modes?"

" Oh, mamma, I was sure you would ask that question! How came it that the lady never asked me that?—And there was something about *fashionable assortment* —She kissed me for reading that; and all the time I did not understand those words. When you kiss me, and praise me, mamma, I feel quite sure, that I have done something well, or good; I know what you are pleased with me for; but I did not know exactly why that lady was so much pleased with me; do you know, mamma?"

" No, my dear; and I am not sure that she was much pleased with you."

" Oh, yes, mamma, I think she really was very much pleased with me, though she was a foolish woman and did not know why."

" Did not know why she was a foolish woman, do you mean ?"

" No, mamma; but did not know why she was pleased with me."

" In that respect," said his mother, laughing, " it seems, that you were as foolish as she was."

" But, mamma," said Frank, " why are not you quite sure, that she liked me ?"

" Because, my dear, I have often heard people tell children, that they were sweet creatures, and charming dears, and clever fellows; and I have observed, that these people forget the charming dears as soon as they are out of sight."

" You and my father never do so:
do you ?"

" Never."

" I had rather, that you and papa
should praise me, and like me, than the
lady I saw in the shop. I think I was
very foolish to tell her what my father
wrote in my book, because I suppose
she did not care about it."

" You will be wiser another time,"
said his mother—" Now put on your
hat, and let us go to look at the bees,
at work in the glass bee-hive."

They went to the old woman's cottage; and the little boy opened the
garden-gate; and Frank went to the
bee-hive, to observe the bees, whilst
his mother sat down in the arbour, and
took a book out of her pocket, in which
she read for some time. It entertained
Frank more, to day, to look at the bees,

than it did the first morning he came
to look at them, because he saw more
distinctly, what they were doing—And
when he had attended to the bees, as
long as he liked, he went to the arbour,
where his mother was sitting; and he
asked her whether he might go and talk
to the little boy, who was now weeding in the garden.

His mother said, that she would rather that he should not talk to this little
boy; but she went to him herself, and
thanked him for letting Frank look at
his bee-hive; and she told him, that, if
he would come to her house, she would
give him a pair of strong shoes.

Then she took Frank by the hand,
and went to the cottage.

Somebody was talking to the old
woman, very eagerly, about washing a
gown.

VOL. I.   P

The person, who was talking, was a maid-servant; and she had a muslin gown in her hand, which, she said, her mistress had desired her to take to be washed.

This old woman was a washer-woman.

" Look here!" said the maid, showing the bottom of the muslin gown, on which there were the marks of shoes, which had trodden upon it, and on which there was the mark of a large hole, that had been mended, " Look here! what a piece of work I have had this morning. Yesterday, my mistress came home with her gown torn and dirtied in this manner; and she told me it was all done by a little mischievous, troublesome, conceited brat of a boy, that she met with in the milliner's shop at ————, where she was yesterday."

Whilst the maid was saying this, she did not see Frank or his mother; for her back was turned towards the door through which they came.

" Oh, mamma!" cried Frank, " I remember, that was the gown the lady had on, who called me a charming little fellow, and who *praised*, I mean the other word, *flattered* me so much; but now she calls me a little mischievous, troublesome, conceited brat, only because I trod upon her gown by accident, and tore it—I did not know I had torn it—I remember I caught my foot in it, when you called me to come away with you. Mamma, if I had torn or dirtied your gown, I do not think you would have been so angry with me. The next time any body begins to flatter me, and to tell me I am *a charming little dear*, I shall recollect all this; and I shall not repeat my verses, nor tell them what papa wrote in my book."

FRANK, who had seen the little boy to whom the bee-hive belonged weeding the beds in the garden, said to his mother one morning, " Mamma, I should like to try to weed some of the borders in your garden, as that little boy weeds the beds in his grandmother's garden."

Frank's mother said, that he might weed one of the borders in her garden; and she lent him a little hoe; and he went to work, and weeded a piece of the border very carefully; and his mother looked at it, when he had done, and said, that it was very well done.

" The same day, at dinner, Frank's father gave him a bit of cheese; and his mother was surprised to see Frank take this cheese off his plate, and put it be-

twixt his fore finger and his middle finger; then he took a piece of bread and
stuck it betwixt his middle finger and his
fourth finger, and then he took a large
mouthful of the cheese, and a large
mouthful of the bread, so that his mouth
was filled in a very disagreeable manner.

" Pray, Frank," said his mother,
" what are you about ? "

Frank's mouth was not empty for
nearly a minute; and he could make no
answer.

" Where did you learn this new method of eating bread and cheese ? "

" Mamma," said Frank, " I saw the
little boy in the cottage eating his bread
and cheese, after he had done weeding; and he ate it just in this way."

" And why should you act in that
way, because you saw him do so ? "

" Mamma, I thought you liked that

little boy; I thought he was a very good boy; do not you remember his bringing me back the bunch of ripe cherries, that I dropped? You called him an honest little fellow; and do not you remember, that he has been very good-natured, in telling us all he knew about bees, and in letting me look at his glass bee-hive? And you know, mamma, this morning, you said, when you saw him at work, that he was very industrious; did not you?"

" Yes, I did; I think he is very industrious, and that he was good natured in letting you look at his glass bee-hive, and honest in returning to you the bunch of ripe cherries, which you dropped: but what has all this to do with his method of eating bread and cheese?"

" I do not know, mamma," said Frank, after thinking a little while —

" Nothing to do with it. But I thought you would be pleased to see me do every thing like him, because you were pleased this morning when you saw me weeding like him."

" You may weed like him," said Frank's mother, " without eating like him; he weeds well, but he eats disagreeably — I shall be glad to see you as honest, and as good-natured, and as industrious as he is; but I should be sorry to see you imitate his manner of eating, because that is disagreeable. Sensible people do not imitate every thing, which they see others do; they imitate only what is useful or agreeable."

Frank took the bread and cheese from betwixt his fore finger and his middle finger, and between his middle finger and his fourth finger; and he put the cheese upon his plate, and did not any longer imitate the manner in which he had seen the little boy in the cottage cram his mouth.

" Did you ever hear," said Frank's father, " of the manner in which apes are sometimes caught?"

" No, papa."

" Apes are apt to imitate every thing which they see done; and they cannot, as you can, Frank, distinguish what is useful and agreeable, from what is useless or disagreeable — they imitate every thing without reflecting. Men, who want to catch these apes, go under the trees in which the apes live; and the men take with them basins with water in them, in which they wash their own hands. They rub their hands, and wash, and wash, for some time, till they perceive, that the apes are looking at them; then the men go away, and carry with them the basins of water; and they leave under the trees large heavy

wooden basins, filled with pitch—You
have seen pitch, Frank: you know, that
it is a very sticky substance. The apes,
as soon as the men are out of sight, come
down from the trees, and go to the basins to wash their hands, in imitation
of the men. The apes dip their hands
into the pitch ; and the pitch sticks to
their hairy hands; and the apes cannot
draw their hands out of the pitch. Now
these animals usually run upon all fours."

" All fours, papa!" interrupted Frank,
" how is that ?"

" As you run, upon your hands and
feet upon the carpet, sometimes.——
The apes cannot run well, for want of
their hands, and because the wooden
bowls, which stick to their hands, are so
heavy. The men, who left these bowls,
come back, and find the apes caught in
this manner."

" I think these apes are very foolish animals," said Frank.

" So do I," said his father: " no animals are wise, who imitate what they see done, without considering the reason why it is done."

FRANK asked his mother, if she would take him again to the cottage garden, to see the bees at work in the glass bee-hive; but his mother answered, " I am afraid to take you there again, till I am sure that you will not imitate the little boy in every thing which you see him do; for instance——"

" Oh, mamma!" said Frank, " I know what you are going to say — But to day, at dinner, you shall see, that I will not eat in that disagreeable way."

His mother attended to him several

days; and when she observed, that he did not imitate this boy any more, in his manner of eating, she took him again to the cottage.

The old woman was spinning; and Frank stopped to look at her spinning-wheel; and he asked his mother, what was the use of what the old woman was doing.

She told him, that the woman was twisting a kind of coarse thread, and that her spinning-wheel was a machine, which helped her to do this quickly.

His mother then asked Frank, whether he knew where the thread was found, or how it was made.

" No, mamma," said Frank.

" It is made of a plant, called flax, my dear," said his mother—" I think you went with me, last summer, through a field in which you saw flax—You took notice of its pretty blue flowers."

Frank said, that he did remember this; but that he could not imagine how the thread, which he saw upon the spinning-wheel, could be made from that green plant with the blue flowers.

His mother told him, that she would show him, whenever she had an opportunity.

The old woman, who was spinning, told Frank's mother, that a neighbour of hers was this very day hackling some flax, and that, if she liked to let Frank see how it was done, she would show her the way to the house where her neighbour lived.

" I should like to see what is meant by hackling flax," said Frank.

" Then come with us, and you shall see," said his mother.

Frank followed his mother to another cottage, where he saw a woman beating, with the edge of a thin bit of wood, something, which he thought looked a little like very yellow dry hay; but his mother told him, that this was flax.

As the woman beat it, a great deal of dust and dirt fell out of it, upon the ground; and, by degrees, the flax, which she held in her hand, looked cleaner and cleaner, and finer and finer, till, at last, it looked like yellow hair.

" But, mamma," said Frank, " the flax, which I saw last summer, growing in a field near this house, had long green stalks and blue flowers; and I saw no yellow threads, like these—Is this a different kind of flax ?"

" No, my dear; this is the same flax. The blue flowers have withered and died. When the blue flowers began to wither, the woman pulled up all the green stalks, and bound them together in bundles, and put these bundles under water, where she left them for about a fortnight; that during this time, the green outside of the stalk decayed, and the stringy part remained; that she then untied the bundles, and spread them out, near a fire, to dry; that, in a few days, they were dried, and then she brought the flax home—And this," said she, showing Frank a bit of the flax, which the woman had not yet beaten and cleaned, " this is the flax as it looks after it has been soaked in water and dried."

" And what is going to be done to it now, mamma?" said Frank, who observed, that the woman was now placing two small boards before her, on which

were stuck, with their points upright,
several rows of steel pins; their points
were as sharp as needles.

" I am going to hackle the flax, master," said the woman: and she began
to comb the flax with these steel combs
—She drew the flax through the steel
pins, several times. The board, into
which the pins were stuck, was fastened
upon the table; and, as the woman
drew the flax through the pins, it was
disentangled, and combed smooth.

" Mamma," said Frank, " it is just
like combing hair out, only the woman
does not move the comb, but she draws
the hair—the flax, I mean, through
it."

The pins in one of the boards were
much smaller, and placed closer together, than those in the other board.

" This is the large comb, and this is

the small-toothed comb, mamma," said
Frank.

And when the flax had been drawn
through these fine pins, there was not
a tangle left in it: and it looked smooth,
bright, and shining, and of a light yellow
colour.

Frank's mother showed him that this
looked the same as what he had seen
on the old woman's spinning-wheel.

They went back to the spinning-
wheel; and the old woman sat down,
and spun a little; and Frank saw, that
the threads of the flax were twisted
together—He did not exactly know
how; and his mother told him, that
he must not expect to find out how it
was done, by looking at it for a few
minutes.

Frank said, " Mamma, I feel tired;
my eyes are tired of looking; and I

am tired with thinking about this spinning-wheel."

" Then do not think any more about it now; go and run in the garden: and Frank ran into the garden; and he jumped and sang; then he listened to the birds, who were singing; and he smelled the flowers, particularly rosemary and balm, which he had never smelled before; and he heard the humming of bees near him, as he was smelling to the rosemary; and he recollected that he had not looked at the bees, this day; so he ran to the glass bee-hive, and watched them working.

And afterwards he ran back to his mother and said, " I am quite rested now, mamma—I mean I do not feel tired of thinking about the spinning-wheel. May I look at the woman spinning again ?"

" Yes, my dear."

Frank went into the cottage, and looked at the old woman, who was spinning.

" Would you like to try to spin a bit, dear?" said the old woman.

" Yes, I should," said Frank; " it looks as if it was very easy to do it; but perhaps it is not; for I remember, I could not plane with the carpenter's plane, though it seemed very easy when he was doing it."

Frank tried to spin, but he broke the thread almost at the first trial; however, the old woman clapped her hands and said, " That's a pretty dear! He spins as well as I do, I declare!"

" Oh, no, no, no," said Frank; " I know I cannot spin at all;" and he looked ashamed, and left the spinning-wheel, and turned away from the old woman, and went back to his mother.

She walked home with him; and, as they were walking home, his mother said to him, " Do you know why you came back just now, Frank?"

" Yes, mamma, because the woman called me pretty dear, and told me, that I could spin as well as she could: and you know I could not; so that was flattering me; and I do not like people that flatter me—I remember the lady in the shop, who flattered me, and afterwards called me a mischievous brat—But I do not much like to think of that.—Mamma, of what use is that brown thread, which the old woman made of the flax?"

" Of that brown thread, linen is made, my dear."

" But linen is white, mamma: how is the brown thread made white?"

" It is left in a place where the sun
shines upon it; and there are other
ways of making linen white, which I
cannot now explain to you. Making
linen white is called bleaching it."

" Can you explain to me, mamma,
how thread is made into linen ?"

" No, my dear, I cannot ; but perhaps your father, when you are able to
understand it, may show you how people weave linen in a loom."

ONE night, when Frank's brother
Henry was with him, they were talking
of Henry's garden.

Henry said, " Next spring, I intend
to sow some scarlet runners, or French
beans, in my garden."

" Whereabouts in your garden ?"
said Frank.

Henry tried to describe to him where-abouts; but Frank could not understand him; so Henry took his pencil out of his pocket and said, " Now, Frank, I will draw for you a map of my garden; and then you will understand it."

He drew the shape of his garden upon paper; and he marked where all the little walks went, and where the rose-bush stood, and where the sally fence was; and he drew all the borders, and printed upon each of the borders the name of what was planted there when Frank last saw it.

Frank, after he had looked at this drawing for a little while, understood it, and saw the exact spot in which Henry intended to sow his scarlet runners.

" So this is what you called a map," said Frank; " but it is not like the maps in papa's study."

" They are maps of countries, not of little gardens," said Henry.

" I suppose they are of the same use to other people, that the little map of your garden was to me—to show them whereabouts places are—But, Henry, what are those odd-shaped, crooked bits of wood, which hook into one another, and which I thought you called a map ?"

" That is a map pasted upon wood; and the shapes of the different places are cut out, through the paper, and through the wood; and then they can be joined together again, exactly in the same shape, that they were in at first."

" I do not understand how you mean," said Frank.

Henry cut out the different beds and walks, in the little map, which he had drawn of his garden ; and when he had separated the parts, he threw them down upon the table, before Frank, and asked him to try if he could put them together again, as they were before.

After some trials, Frank did join them all together; and he told Henry, that he should very much like to try to put his wooden map together, and that he would be very much obliged to him, if he would lend it to him.

" I am afraid," said Henry, " to lend you that map, lest you should lose any of the parts of it."

" I will not lose them, I assure you."

" I tried every day for a week," said Henry, " before I was able to put it all together; and after I had done with it every day, I put it into the box belonging to it; and I regularly counted all the bits, to see that I had them right."

" I will count them every day, before

I put them by, if you will lend them to me," said Frank.

"If you will promise me to do so," said Henry, "I will lend you my map for a week."

Frank was eagerly going to say "*Yes, I will promise you*," when he felt a hand before his lips—It was his mother's—" My dear Frank," said she, in a serious tone of voice, " consider before you ever make any promise—No persons are believed, or trusted, who break their promise—You are very young, Frank; and you scarcely know what a promise means."

"I think I know, mamma, what this promise means," said Frank.

" And do you think you shall be able to keep your promise?"

" Yes, mamma," said Frank, " I hope that I shall."

" I hope so too, my dear," said his mother; " for I would rather, that you should never put that map together, than that you should make a promise and break it."

Frank promised Henry, that whenever he took the map out of the box, he would count the pieces, to see whether he had the right number, before he put them again into the box.

" Remember," said Frank, " I do not promise, that I will not lose any of the pieces of the map—I promise only to count them; but I hope I shall not lose any of them.

Henry told him, that he understood very well what he said; and he put the box into his hands.

Frank immediately counted the pieces of the map—It was a map of England and Wales; and there were fifty-

two pieces; one to represent each
county.

"Fifty-two—fifty-two—fifty-two,"
repeated Frank, several times; "I am
afraid I shall forget how many there
are."

"Then," said Henry, "you had better write it down—Here is a pencil
for you, and you may write it upon the
lid of the box."

Frank wrote a two, and a five after
it.

"That is not right," said Henry;
"that is twenty-five; and you know
that there are fifty-two."

"Then," said Frank, "I must put
the five to my left hand, and the two
to my right hand, to make fifty-two.
—Mamma, I did not understand, what
papa told me once, about the places of
units, and tens, and hundreds."

" Then you had better ask him to explain it to you again, when he is at leisure: for want of knowing this, when you were to write fifty-two, you wrote twenty-five."

' " That was a great mistake: but papa is busy now, and cannot explain about units and tens to me; therefore, I will put the map together, if I can."

Frank could not put the map together the first night that he tried, nor the second day, nor the third: but he regularly remembered to count the bits, according to his promise, every day, before he put them into the box.

One day, he was in a great hurry to go out to fly his kite; but all the pieces of the map were scattered upon the carpet: and he staid to count them, and put them into the box, before he went out.

It was not easy to get them into the

box, which was but just large enough to hold them when they were well packed.

The lid of the box would not slide into its place, when the pieces of the map were not put in so as to lie quite flat.

One day—it was Friday—Frank saw his father open a large book, in which there were very pretty prints of houses; and he was eager to go to look at these prints; but his map was upon the table; and he thought he had better count the pieces, and put them into the box, before he went to look at the prints, lest he should forget to do it afterwards: therefore, he counted them as fast as he could —They were not all right—Fifty-two was the number, that had been lent to him; and he could find but fifty-one.

He searched all over the room—un-

der the tables—under the chairs—upon
the sofa—under the cushions of the sofa
—under the carpet—everywhere he
could think of. The lost bit of the map
was nowhere to be found; and, whilst
he was searching, his father turned over
all the leaves in the book of prints, found
the print that he wanted, then shut the
book and put it into its place in the
book-case.

Frank was, at this instant, crawling
from beneath the sofa, where he had
been feeling for his lost county—He
looked up and sighed, when he saw the
book of pretty prints shut and put up
into the book-case.

" Oh, papa ! there is the very thing
I have been looking for all this time,"
cried Frank, who now espied the bit of
the map, which he had missed: it was
lying upon the table; and the book of

prints had been put upon it, so that Frank never could see it till the book was lifted up.

" I am glad I have found you, little crooked county of Middlesex," said Frank—" Now I have them all right —fifty-two."

The next morning—Saturday—the last day of the week during which the map was lent to Frank, he spent an hour and a half* in trying to put it together; at last he succeeded, and hooked every county, even crooked little Middlesex, into its right place.

He was much pleased to see the whole map fitted together—" Look at it, dear mamma," said he: " you cannot see the joinings, it fits so nicely."

---

* A boy of four years old, spent, voluntarily, above an hour and a half, in attempts to put together a joining map.

His mother was just come to look at his map, when they heard a noise of several sheep ba-a-ing very loud near the windows. Frank ran to the window, and he saw a large flock of sheep passing near the window; a man and two women were driving them.

"How fat they look, mamma!" said Frank; "they seem as if they could hardly walk, they are so fat."

"They have a great deal of wool upon their backs."

"Mamma, what can be the use of those large, very large, scissars, which that woman carries in her hand?"

"Those large scissars are called shears; and with them the wool will be cut from the backs of these sheep."

"Will it hurt the sheep, mamma, to cut their wool off?"

"Not at all, I believe."

" I should like, then, to see it done;
and I should like to touch the wool.
What use is made of wool, mamma ?"

" Your coat is made of wool, my
dear."

Frank looked surprised; and he was
going to ask how wool could be made
into a coat; but his father came into
the room, and asked him if he should
like to go with him to see some sheep
sheared.

" Yes, very much, papa; thank you,"
said Frank, jumping down from the
chair on which he stood.

" I shall be ready to go in five minutes," said his father.

"I am ready this minute," said Frank;
" I have nothing to do, but to get my
hat, and to put on my shoes."—But,
just as he got to the door, he recollected,
that he had left Henry's map upon the

floor; and he returned back, and was going hastily to put it into the box; but he then recollected his promise, to count the pieces every day, before he put them into the box. He was much afraid, that his father should be ready before he had finished counting them, and that he should be left behind, and should not see the sheep sheared; but he kept his promise exactly: he counted the fifty-two pieces, put them into the box, and was ready the instant his father called him.

He saw the wool cut off the backs of the sheep; it did not entertain him quite so much as he had expected to see this done; but, when he returned home, he was very glad to meet his brother Henry in the evening; and he returned the box of maps to him.

"Thank you, Henry," said he;

" here is your map, safe—Count the pieces, and you will find, that there are fifty-two—And I have kept my promise: I have counted them every day, before I put them into the box—My mother saw me count them every day." ·

" I am glad, Frank, that you have kept your promise," said Henry, and his mother, and his father, all at once; and they all looked pleased with him.

His father took down the book of pretty prints, and put it into Frank's hands.

" I will lend you this book for a week," said his father; " you may look at all the prints in it; I can trust you with it; for I saw, that you took care of Henry's map, which was lent to you."

Frank opened the book, and he saw, upon the first page, the print of the front of a house.

"The reason I wished to look at this book so much," said Frank, "was, because I thought I saw prints of houses in it; and I am going to build a house in my garden.

"You have kept your promise so well," said Henry, "about the map, that I will lend you—what I would not lend to any body, that I could not trust—I will lend you my box full of little bricks, if you will not take them out of doors, nor wet them."

Frank said, that he would not either take them out of doors, or wet them.

And Henry believed that Frank would do what he said that he would do, because he had kept his promise exactly with respect to the map.

Frank received the box full of little bricks, with a joyful countenance; and his mother gave him leave to build with them, in the room in which he slept.

Henry showed him how to *break the joints*, in building—how to build walls and arches—And Frank was happy in building different sorts of buildings, and stair-cases, and pillars, and towers, and arches, with the little bricks, which were lent to him—And he kept his promise, not to wet them and not to take them out of doors.

" It is a good thing to keep one's promise," said his mother : " people are trusted, who keep their promises— trusted even with little bricks * ."

---

* These little bricks were made of plaster of Paris : they were *exactly* twice as long as they were broad, and twice as broad as they were thick. Two inches and a quarter long, is a convenient length, being one quarter of the length of a common brick. Common bricks are not exactly in

It was autumn—The leaves withered and fell from the trees; and the paths in the grove were strewed with the red leaves of the beech trees.

Little Frank swept away the leaves in his mother's favourite walk in the grove: it was his morning's work to make this walk quite clean; and, as soon as dinner was over, he slid down from his chair; and he went to his mother, and asked her if she would walk out this evening in the grove.

" I think," said his mother, " it is now too late in the year, to walk after dinner: the evenings are cold; and—"

the proportion above mentioned, as there is generally allowance made for mortar. A few lintels of wood, the depth and breadth of a brick, and twelve inches and three quarters long, will be found very convenient: these should be painted exactly to match the colour of the bricks.

" Oh, mamma," interrupted Frank,
" pray walk out, this one evening —
Look, the sun has not set yet; look at
the pretty red sun-shine upon the tops
of the trees—Several of the trees in the
grove have leaves upon them still, mamma, and I have swept away all the
withered leaves, that were strewed upon
your path—Will you come and look
at it, mamma?"

" Since you have swept my path,
and have taken pains to oblige me,"
said his mother, " I will walk with you,
Frank—People should not always do
just what they like best themselves:
they should be sometimes ready to comply with the wishes of their friends;
so, Frank, I will comply with your wish
and walk to the grove."

His mother found it a more pleasant
evening than she had expected; and

the walk in the grove was sheltered;
and she thanked Frank for having
swept it.

The wind had blown a few leaves
from one of the heaps, which he had
made; and he ran on before his mother to clear them away—But, as he
stooped to brush away one of the leaves,
he saw a caterpillar, which was so nearly
the colour of the faded green leaf upon
which it lay, that he, at first sight, mistook it for a part of the leaf—It stuck
to the leaf, and did not move in the
least, even when Frank touched it—
He carried it to his mother, and asked
her if she thought that it was dead,
or if she knew what was the matter
with it.

"I believe, my dear," said his mother, "that this caterpillar will soon
turn into a chrysalis."

" Chry——what, mamma?"

" Chrysalis."

" What is a chrysalis?"

" I cannot describe it to you; but, if you keep this caterpillar a few days, you will see what I mean by a chrysalis."

" I will—But how do you know, mamma, that a eaterpillar will turn into a chrysalis?"

" I have seen caterpillars, that have turned into chrysalises; and I have heard, that they do so, from many other people, who have seen it; and I have read, in books, accounts of caterpillars, that have turned into chrysalises: and this is the time of the year in which, as it has been observed, this change usually happens."

" But, my dear mother," said Frank, " may I keep this caterpillar in my red box?—And what shall I give it to eat?"

"You need not give it any thing to eat; for it will not eat whilst it is in this state: and you may keep this caterpillar in your box; it will soon become a chrysalis; and, in the spring, a moth, or butterfly, will come out of the chrysalis."

Frank looked much surprised at hearing this; and he said, that he would take great care of the caterpillar, and that he would watch it, that he might see all these curious changes.

"Who was the first person, mamma, that ever observed that a caterpillar turned into a chrysalis, and a chrysalis into a butterfly?"

"I don't know, my dear."

"Mamma, perhaps, if I observe, I may find out things, as well as other people."

" Yes, very likely you may."

" Mamma, how did the person, who wrote about animals, in my book, that my father gave me, find out all that he knew ?"

" Partly from reading other books, and partly from observing animals him-self."

" But, mamma," said Frank, " how did the people, who wrote the other books, know all the things, that are told in them ?"

" By observing," said his mother—" Different people, in different places, observed different animals, and wrote the histories of those animals."

" I am very glad that they did.— Did they ever make mistakes, mamma ?"

" Yes, I believe, that they did make a great many mistakes."

" Then every thing, that is in books, is not true, is it ?"

" No."

" I am sorry for that—But how shall I know what is true, and what is not true, in books, mamma ?"

" You cannot always find out what is true, and what is not true, in books, till you have more knowledge, my dear."

" And how shall I get more knowledge, mamma ?"

" By observing whatever you see, and hear, and feel; by reading; and by trying experiments."

" Experiments, mamma!—Papa and grown-up wise people try experiments; but I did not know, that such a little boy as I am could try experiments."

Frank and his mother had walked on, whilst they were talking, till they came to a path, which led to the river side.

A little girl was by the river side,

dipping a yellow earthen jug into the water.

The girl did not perceive Frank and his mother, who were coming behind her, till she heard Frank's voice, which startled her; and she let the pitcher fall from her hand and it broke.

The girl looked very sorry, that she had broke the jug; but a woman, who was standing beside her, said, " It is no great misfortune, Mary; for we can take it home, and tie it together, and boil it in milk, and it will be as good as ever."

" My dear mother," cried Frank, " then we can mend the broken flower-pot—Shall we do it as soon as we get home ?"

" We can *try* to do it as soon as we go home."

" *Try*, mamma! But are not you sure it will do ? That woman said, the jug would be as good as ever, if it was tied together and boiled in milk."

" Yes; but she may be mistaken— We had better try the experiment ourselves."

" Is that called trying an experiment?"

" Yes, this is an experiment we can try."

When they got home, Frank's mother rang the bell, and asked to have a clean saucepan and some milk up stairs; and when the saucepan was brought to her, she tied the pieces of the broken flowerpot together, with packthread, in the same shape that it was before it was broken—She put the flower-pot into the saucepan; and she poured over it as much milk as entirely covered it; and, after she had put the saucepan on the fire, she waited till the milk boiled, then she took the saucepan off the fire; and she waited till the milk grew so cool, that she could dip her fingers into it, without burning herself; and she took out the flower-pot, and carefully untied the wet packthread, and unwound it; but, when she had unwound it, the parts of the flower-pot did not stick together: they separated; and Frank was disappointed.

"But, mamma," said he, "I wish you would be so good as to send to the woman, and ask her how it was that she could mend broken things by boiling them in milk; perhaps she knows something about it, that we do not know yet."

"Stay," said Henry: "before you send to the woman, try another experiment—Here's a saucer, which I broke just before you came in from walking— I was rubbing some Indian ink upon it, and I let it slip off the table—Let us tie this together, and try whether you can mend it by boiling it in the milk."

The saucer was tied together; the milk, that was in the saucepan, was poured out; and some cold milk was put into it; into this milk the saucer was put; and the milk was then boiled; and the moment the saucepan was taken off the fire, Frank was impatient to see the saucer. Before it was nearly cool, he untied the string; the parts of the saucer did not stick together; and Frank was more disappointed now than he had been before.

His mother smiled and said, " Frank, people, who wish to try experiments, you see, must be patient."

The woman, whom he had heard speaking to the little girl by the river side, lived very near to them; and

Frank's mother sent to beg to speak to her—She came; and, when she was told what had been done about the flower-pot and the saucer, she asked whether it was a long time since the flower-pot had been broken.

" Yes, about two months."

" Then, ma'am," said she, " that could not be mended this way—I can only mend things this way, that have been fresh broken."

" Mamma," said Frank, " how comes it, that the saucer, which Henry did but just break before we came in from walking, did not stick together, after all we did to it ?"

" Perhaps, master," said the woman, " you did not let it stand to cool before you untied it."

" No, I did not," said Frank.

" But, master, you must have patience, and wait till it is quite cool, or it will never do."

" I will be more patient this time, mamma, if you will let me try once more."

His mother let him try once more; and Frank was going to boil the milk again, but the old woman said, that the milk which had been boiled, would not *do*, and that he must use new milk.

And Frank said, " This will waste a great deal of milk."

But the old woman said, " I never waste the milk; for I give it to the children afterwards, or to the chickens, and I do not throw it away."

Frank now began to tie the broken saucer together, and the old woman said to him, " Fit it very close and even, and tie it very tight, or it will not do."

"I have tied it as tight as I can," said Frank.

"But, master, it is not nearly tight enough," said the woman: "I will show you how to tighten it better, if you will give me a small wooden skewer, or a bit of wood, that I can cut into a skewer, about the size of your pencil.

"Here is such a bit of wood as you want," said Frank's mother.

"Now, master," said the old woman, "take another piece of packthread, and wind it three times round the saucer, and tie the ends together. Leave it quite loose, so that you may put your finger between the saucer and the pack-thread —— Very well — Now, master, put this stick between the packthread and the saucer, and twist the pack-thread tight with the stick."

" The packthread looks like a screw as I twist it," said Frank.

" Yes," said his mother, " and you see that you really screw the parts of the saucer together."

" Yes," said Frank, " and this is as tight and as strong as the stick and string in my skip-jack, and it is something like it; is it not, mamma?"

" Yes, my dear."

" I will run for my skip-jack, and see whether it is quite the same," said Frank.

" You had better finish what you are about first," said his mother. " You can look at the skip-jack after-wards. — Do one thing at a time, my dear."

Frank boiled the new milk, and put the well-tied saucer into it, and this time he waited till the saucer was cool, and then he untied the string; and he found, that the parts of the saucer stuck fast together; and he could scarcely see the place where they were joined.

He was pleased with this success, and he said, " People must be patient, who try experiments ; and people must be patient, who are to observe things ; so I will have patience till next spring, and then I shall see the chrysalis change to a moth or a butterfly. But, mother, first I shall see the caterpillar change to a chrysalis."

Frank put his green caterpillar into his red box; and then he went again to look at the saucer, which had been mended, and at the flower-pot, which the old woman said could not be mended; and he asked his mother if she could tell the reason why things, which had been broken a long time before, could not be mended by being boiled, in this manner, in milk.

" I think I can guess the reason," said his mother; " but I will not tell it to you; I would rather, that you should think and find it out for yourself. If I were to tell you the reason of every thing, my dear, you would never take the trouble of thinking for yourself; and you know I shall not always be with you, to *think* for you."

———

" MAMMA," said Frank, " there is a reason that I have thought of; but I am not sure, that it is the right reason —but it may be one of the reasons."

" Well, let us hear it, without any more *reasons*," said his mother, laughing.

" I thought, mamma," said Frank, " that, perhaps, the old woman could never mend things——"

" Things! what sort of things; chairs and tables, or coats and waistcoats?"

" Oh, mamma, you know very well what I mean."

" Yes, I guess what you mean; but other people will not be at the trouble of guessing at the meaning of what you say; therefore, if you wish to be understood, you must learn to explain yourself distinctly."

" I thought, mamma," said Frank, " that the reason why the old woman could never mend cups and saucers, or jugs, or plates, that had been broken a great while, was, because, perhaps, the edges of these might have been rubbed, or broken off, so that they could not be fitted close together again. If you recollect, the old woman said to me, when I was tying the broken saucer together, ' Tie it tight, and fit it close, or it will not do.'——Do you think, that I have found out the right reason, mamma? Is it the reason which you thought of?"

" It is the reason," answered his mother, " which I thought of; but my having thought of it is no proof that it is right. The best way to find out whether this is the case is to try.—— Can you find out, yourself, Frank, how you may prove whether this is the reason or not?"

" I would rub the edges of a plate, or saucer, after it was broken; and, when I had rubbed off little bits of the edges, I would tie the pieces together and boil them in milk; and 1 would, at the same time, break another bit of

the same plate, or saucer; and I would
tie the broken pieces together, without
rubbing off any of the edges, and I
would put it into the same milk; and
let it be upon the fire as long, and let
it be as long before I untied it, as before
I untied the other broken pieces; and
then we should see whether the rubbing
off the edges would prevent the pieces
from joining or not."

Frank's mother told him, that he might
try his experiment.—He tried it; and
he found, that the broken bits of the plate,
whose edges he had broken off, could
not be joined by being boiled in milk;
and two other broken bits of the same
plate, which he joined without rubbing
off their edges, stuck together, after they
had been boiled in milk, very well.

Then Frank said, " Mamma, there
is another thing, which I should like to

try; I should like to tie the broken flower-pot very tight together, and to fit the pieces closely; for the last time I tied it, I did not tie it very tight: I did not know, that I should have done that, till the old woman told me that I should. I think, perhaps, the flower-pot may be mended, because, though it has been broken a great while, the edges of it have never been rubbed, I believe; it has been lying in the press, in your room; and nobody has ever meddled with it."

" Nobody has ever meddled with it, I believe," said his mother; "for I lock that press every day; and no one goes to it but myself; and I have never rubbed any thing against the edges of the broken flower-pot."

She went and brought the pieces of the broken flower-pot; and Frank tied

them together very tight, after he had
fitted their edges closely and evenly together. He boiled this flower-pot again
in milk, waited afterwards till it became
cool, and then untied it, and he found,
that the parts stuck together; and he
poured water into it, and the water did
not run out. Frank was glad, that he
had mended the flower-pot at last.

"Do you think, mother," said he,
"that it was made to stick together
again by being tied so tight, or by the
milk, or by both together?"

"I do not know," answered his mother; "but you may try whether tying
broken pieces of earthen-ware together
will fasten them, without boiling them
in milk."

Frank tried this; and he let the pieces
that were tied together remain still as
long as those, which he had before

boiled in milk; and when he untied the string, the pieces separated: they did not stick together in the least.—He afterwards tied these pieces together again, and boiled them in water; and he found, when he untied them, that they did not stick together.

———

THERE was one part of the winter's evening which Frank liked particularly; it was the half hour after dinner, when the window shutters were shut, and the curtains let down, and the fire stirred, so as to make a cheerful blaze, which lighted the whole room.

His father and mother did not ring the bell for candles, because they liked to sit a little while after dinner, by the light of the fire.

Frank's father used often, at this

time, to play with him, or to talk to him.

One evening, after his father had been playing with Frank, and had made him jump, and run, and wrestle, and laugh, till Frank was quite hot, and out of breath, he knelt down upon the carpet, at his father's feet, rested his arms upon his father's knees, and looking up in his face, he said, " Now, papa, whilst I am resting myself so happily here, will you tell me something entertaining ?"

But just as Frank said the word *entertaining*, the door opened, and the servant came into the room with lighted candles.

" Oh, candles! I am sorry you are come!" cried Frank.

" Oh, candles! I am glad you have come," said his father; " for now I can see to read an entertaining book, which I want to finish."

" But, papa," said Frank, " cannot you sit still, a *little, little* while longer, and tell me some short thing?"

" Well, what shall I tell you?"

" There are so many things, that I want to know, papa, I do not know which to ask for first — I want to know whether you have ever seen a camel — and I want to know where silk-worms are found, and how they make silk — and I want to know how people weave linen in a loom, and how the wool of sheep is made into such coats as we have on — And, oh, father! I wish, very much, to know how the fat of animals is made into candles — You promised to tell me, or to show me, how that was done — And, oh! more than all the rest, I wish to know how

plates, and jugs, and cups and saucers,
and flower-pots, are made of clay—and
whether they are made of clay such as
I have in my garden—And I want very
much, to know where tea comes from
—and———"

" Stop, stop ! my dear Frank," said
his father ; " it would take up a great
deal more of my time, than I can be-
stow upon you, to answer all these questions—I cannot answer any of them to
night, for I have a great many other
things to do—The first thing you asked
me, I think, was whether I had ever
seen a camel—I have ; and the print I
am going to show you is very like the
animal that I saw ; and you may read
his history ; and then you will know all
that I know of camels ; and, when you
have satisfied your curiosity about camels, I can lend you another book, in

which you may read the history of silk-
worms."

"Thank you, papa," said Frank:
"I shall like to read these things, very
much; only I cannot read quick yet,
papa; and there are words, sometimes,
which I cannot make out well."

"If you persevere," said his father,
"you will soon be able to read without
any difficulty—But nothing can be done
well without perseverance—You have
showed me, that you have a great deal
of perseverance, and——"

"Have I, papa?" interrupted Frank,
"when did I show that to you?"

"The morning when you tried, for
an hour and a half, to put the joining
map together."

"And at last I did put it together."

"Yes; you succeeded, because you
persevered."

" Then," said Frank, " I will persevere, and learn to read easily, that I
may read all the entertaining things that
are in books ; and then I shall be as glad,
when the candles come, as you were,
just now, papa."

LITTLE DOG TRUSTY;

LIAR AND THE BOY OF TRUTH.

———

FRANK and Robert were two little boys, about eight years old.

Whenever Frank did any thing wrong, he always told his father and mother of it; and when any body asked him about any thing, which he had done or said, he always told the truth; so that every body, who knew him, believed him: but nobody, who knew his brother Robert, believed a word which he said, because he used to tell lies.

Whenever he did any thing wrong,

he never ran to his father and mother to tell them of it; but when they asked him about it, he denied it, and said he had not done the things which he had done.

The reason that Robert told lies was because he was afraid of being punished for his faults, if he confessed them. He was a coward, and could not bear the least pain; but Frank was a brave boy, and could bear to be punished for little faults; his mother never punished him so much for such little faults as she did Robert for the lies which he told, and which she found out afterward.

One evening, these two little boys were playing together, in a room by themselves; their mother was ironing in a room next to them, and their father was out at work in the fields, so there was nobody in the room with Robert and Frank; but there was a little dog, Trusty, lying by the fireside.

Trusty was a pretty playful little dog, and the children were very fond of him.

" Come," said Robert to Frank, " there is Trusty lying beside the fire, asleep; let us go and waken him, and he will play with us."

" O yes, do, let us," said Frank. So they both ran together towards the hearth, to waken the dog.

Now there was a basin of milk standing upon the hearth; and the little boys did not see whereabouts it stood; for it was behind them; as they were both playing with the dog, they kicked it with their feet, and threw it down; and the basin broke, and all the milk ran out of it over the hearth and about the floor : and, when the little boys saw what they had done, they were very sorry and frightened ; but they did not know what to do : they stood, for some time, looking at the broken basin and the milk, without speaking.

Robert spoke first.

" So, we shall have no milk for supper to night," said he; and he sighed——

" No milk for supper ! — why not?" said Frank ; " is there no more milk in the house?"

" Yes, but we shall have none of it ; for do not you remember, last Monday, when we threw down the milk, my mother said, we were very careless, and that the next time we did so, we should have no more ; and this is the next time; so we shall have no milk for supper to night."

"Well, then," said Frank, "we must do without it, that's all, we will take more care another time; there's no great harm done; come, let us run and tell my mother. You know she bid us always tell her directly, when we broke any thing; so come," said he, taking hold of his brother's hand.

"I will come, just now," said Robert; "don't be in such a hurry, Frank—Can't you stay a minute?" So Frank staid; and then he said, "Come now, Robert." But Robert answered, "Stay a little longer; for I dare not go yet—I am afraid."

Little boys, I advise you never be afraid to tell the truth; never say, "*Stay a minute*," and "*Stay a little longer*," but run directly and tell of

what you have done, that is wrong.
The longer you stay, the more afraid
you will grow; till at last, perhaps, you
will not dare to tell the truth at all.
Hear what happened to Robert—

The longer he staid, the more un-
willing he was to go to tell his mother,
that he had thrown the milk down;
and at last he pulled his hand away
from his brother, and cried, " I won't
go at all: Frank, can't you go by yourself?"

" Yes," said Frank, " so I will; I
am not afraid to go by myself; I only
waited for you out of good-nature,
because I thought you would like to
tell the truth too."

" Yes, so I will; I mean to tell
the truth, when I am asked; but I
need not go now, when I do not choose
it; and why need you go either?

Can't you wait here? Surely my mother can see the milk when she comes in."

Frank said no more; but, as his brother would not come, he went without him. He opened the door of the next room, where he thought his mother was ironing; but when he went in he saw that she was gone; and he thought she was gone to fetch some more clothes to iron. The clothes, he knew, were hanging on the bushes in the garden; so he thought his mother was gone there; and he ran after her, to tell what had happened.

Now, whilst Frank was gone, Robert was left in the room by himself; and all the while he was alone he was thinking of some excuses to make to his mother; and he was sorry, that

Frank was gone to tell her the truth. He said to himself, " If Frank and I both were to say, that we did not throw down the basin, she would believe us, and we should have milk for supper. I am very sorry Frank would go to tell her about it."

Just as he said this to himself, he heard his mother coming down stairs— " Oh ho!" said he to himself, " then my mother has not been out in the garden ; and so Frank has not met her, and cannot have told her; so now I may say what I please."

Then this naughty, cowardly boy, determined to tell his mother a lie.

She came into the room ; but when she saw the broken basin, and the milk spilled, she stopped short, and cried, " So, so — What a piece of work is here ! — Who did this, Robert ?"

" I don't know, ma'am," said Robert, in a very low voice.

" You don't know, Robert!—tell me the truth—I shall not be angry with you, child—You will only lose the milk at supper; and as for the basin, I would rather have you break all the basins I have, than tell me one lie. So don't tell me a lie. I ask you, Robert, did you break the basin ?"

" *No, ma'am,* I did not," said Robert; and he coloured as red as fire.

" Then where's Frank ?—did he do it ?"

" No, mother, he did not," said Robert; for he was in hopes, that when Frank came in, he should persuade him to say, that he did not do it.

" How do you know," said his mother, " that Frank did not do it ?"

VOL. I.   X

" Because — because — because, ma'am," said Robert, hesitating, as liars do for an excuse — " because I was in the room all the time, and I did not see him do it."

" Then how was the basin thrown down? If you have been in the room all the time, you can tell."

Then Robert, going on from one lie to another, answered, " I suppose the dog must have done it."

" Did you see him do it?" said his mother?

" Yes," said this wicked boy.

" Trusty, Trusty," said his mother, turning round; and Trusty, who was lying before the fire drying his legs, which were wet with the milk, jumped up and came to her. Then she said, " Fie! fie! Trusty!" pointing to the milk. " Get me a switch out of the garden, Robert; Trusty must be beat for this."

Robert ran for the switch, and in the garden he met his brother: he stopped him and told him, in a great hurry, all that he had said to his mother; and he begged of him not to tell the truth, but to say the same as he had done.

"No, I will not tell a lie," said Frank. "What! and is Trusty to be beat! He did not throw down the milk, and he shan't be beat for it— Let me go to my mother."

They both ran towards the house— Robert got first home, and he locked the house door, that Frank might not come in. He gave the switch to his mother.

Poor Trusty! he looked up as the switch was lifted over his head; but *he* could not speak, to tell the truth. Just as the blow was falling upon him, Frank's voice was heard at the window.

" Stop, stop! dear mother, stop!" cried he, as loud as ever he could call; " Trusty did not do it—let me in—I and Robert did it—but do not beat Robert."

" Let us in, let us in," cried another voice, which Robert knew to be his father's, " I am just come from work, and here's the door locked."

Robert turned as pale as ashes, when he heard his father's voice; for his father always whipped him when he told a lie.

His mother went to the door, and unlocked it.

" What's all this?" cried his father, as he came in: so his mother told him all that had happened.

" Where is the switch, with which you were going to beat Trusty?" said their father.

Then Robert, who saw, by his father's looks, that he was going to beat him, fell upon his knees, and cried for mercy, saying, " Forgive me this time, and I will never tell a lie again."

But his father caught hold of him by the arm—" I will whip you now," said he, " and then, I hope, you will not." So Robert was whipped, till he cried so loud with the pain, that the whole neighbourhood could hear him.

" There," said his father, when he had done, " now go without supper; you are to have no milk to night, and you have been whipped. See how liars are served!" Then turning to Frank, " Come here and shake hands

X 3

with me, Frank; you will have no milk for supper; but that does not signify; you have told the truth, and have not been whipped, and every body is pleased with you. And now I'll tell you what I will do for you—I will give you the little dog Trusty, to be your own dog. You shall feed him, and take care of him, and he shall be your dog: you have saved him a beating; and I'll answer for it you'll be a good master to him. Trusty, Trusty, come here."

Trusty came. Then Frank's father took off Trusty's collar. "To-morrow I'll go to the brazier's," added he, " and get a new collar made for your dog: from this day forward he shall always be called after you, *Frank!* And, wife, whenever any of the neighbours' children ask you why the dog *Trusty* is to be called *Frank*, tell them this story of our two boys: let them know the difference between a liar and a boy of truth."

ORANGE MAN;

HONEST BOY AND THE THIEF.

CHARLES was the name of the honest boy; and Ned was the name of the thief.

Charles never touched what was not his own : *this* is being an honest boy.

Ned often took what was not his own : *this* is being a thief.

Charles's father and mother, when he was a very little boy, had taught him to be honest, by always punishing him when he meddled with what was not his own : but when Ned took what was not his own, his father and mother did not punish him; so he grew up to be a thief.

Early one summer's morning, as Charles was going along the road to school, he met a man leading a horse, which was laden with panniers.

The man stopped at the door of a public-house, which was by the road side; and he said to the landlord, who came to the door, "I won't have my horse unloaded; I shall only stop with you whilst I eat my breakfast. Give my horse to some one to hold here on the road, and let the horse have a little hay to eat."

The landlord called; but there was no one in the way; so he beckoned to Charles, who was going by, and begged him to hold the horse.

"Oh," said the man, "but can you engage him to be an honest boy? for these are oranges in my baskets ; and it is not every little boy one can leave with oranges."

" Yes," said the landlord ; " I have known Charles from the cradle up- wards, and I never caught him in a lie or a theft ; all the parish knows him to be an honest boy ; I'll engage your oranges will be as safe with him as if you were by yourself."

" Can you so ?" said the orange man ; " then I'll engage, my lad, to give you the finest orange in my basket, when I come from breakfast, if you'll watch the rest whilst I am away."

" Yes," said Charles, " I *will* take care of your oranges."

So the man put the bridle into his hand, and he went into the house to eat his breakfast.

Charles had watched the horse and

the oranges about five minutes, when he saw one of his school-fellows coming towards him. As he came nearer, Charles saw that it was Ned.

Ned stopped as he passed, and said, " Good-morrow to you, Charles; what are you doing there? whose horse is that? and what have you got in the baskets?"

" There are oranges in the baskets," said Charles; " and a man, who has just gone into the inn here, to eat his breakfast, bid me take care of them, and so I did; because he said, he would give me an orange, when he came back again."

" An orange," cried Ned; " are you to have a whole orange? I wish I was to have one! However, let me look how large they are." Saying this, Ned went towards the pannier, and lifted up the cloth that covered it. "La! what fine oranges!" he exclaimed, the moment he saw them. "Let me touch them, to feel if they are ripe."

"No," said Charles, "you had better not; what signifies it to you whether they are ripe, you know, since you are not to eat them. You should not meddle with them; they are not yours —You must not touch them."

"Not touch them! Surely," said Ned, "there's no harm in *touching* them. You don't think I mean to steal them, I suppose." So Ned put his hand into the orange man's basket, and he took up an orange, and he felt it; and, when he had felt it, he smelled it. "It smells very sweet," said he, "and it feels very ripe; I long to taste it; I will only just suck one drop of juice at the top." Saying these words, he put the orange to his mouth.

Little boys, who wish to be honest, beware of temptation. People are led on, by little and little, to do wrong.

The *sight* of the oranges tempted Ned to *touch* them; the touch tempted him to *smell* them; and the smell tempted him to *taste* them.

" What are you about, Ned?" cried Charles, taking hold of his arm. " You said, you only wanted to smell the orange; do put it down, for shame!"

" Don't say *for shame* to me," cried Ned, in a surly tone; " the oranges are not yours, Charles !"

" No, they are not mine; but I promised to take care of them, and so I will: so put down that orange ?"

" Oh, if it comes to that, I won't," said Ned, " and let us see, who can make me, if I don't choose it; I'm stronger than you."

" I am not afraid of you, for all that," replied Charles, " for I am in the right." Then he snatched the orange out of Ned's hand, and he pushed him with all his force from the basket.

Ned immediately returned, hit him a violent blow, which almost stunned him.

Still, however, this good boy, without minding the pain, persevered in defending what was left in his care: he still held the bridle with one hand, and covered the basket with his other arm, as well as he could. ―

Ned struggled in vain to get his hands into the pannier again; he could not; and, finding that he could not win by strength, he had recourse to cunning. So he pretended to be out of breath and to desist; but he meant, as soon as Charles looked away, to creep softly round to the basket on the other side.

Cunning people, though they think themselves very wise, are almost always very silly.

Ned, intent upon one thing—the getting round to steal the oranges—forgot, that, if he went too close to the horse's heels, he should startle him. The horse, indeed, disturbed by the bustle near him, had already left off eating his hay, and began to put down his ears; but, when he felt something touch his hind legs, he gave a sudden kick, and Ned fell backwards, just as he had seized the orange.

Ned screamed with the pain; and at the scream all the people came out of the public house to see what was the matter; and amongst them came the orange man.

Ned was now so much ashamed, that he almost forgot the pain, and wished to run away; but he was so much hurt, that he was obliged to sit down again.

The truth of the matter was soon told by Charles, and as soon believed by all the people present, who knew him; for he had the character of being an honest boy; and Ned was known to be a thief and a liar.

So nobody pitied Ned for the pain he felt. " He deserves it," says one; " why did he meddle with what was not his own?" " Pugh; he is not much hurt, I'll answer for it," said another. " And, if he was, it's a lucky kick for him, if it keeps him from the gallows," says a third. Charles was the only person, who said nothing; he helped Ned away to a bank: for boys, that are brave, are always good-natured.

"Oh, come here," said the orange man, calling him: " come here, my honest lad! What! you got that black eye in keeping my oranges, did you? That's a stout little fellow," said he, taking him by the hand and leading him into the midst of the people.

Men, women, and children had gathered around, and all the children fixed their eyes upon Charles, and wished to be in his place.

In the mean time, the orange man took Charles's hat off his head, and filled it with fine China oranges. "There, my little friend," said he, " take them, and God bless you with them! If I could but afford it, you should have all that is in my baskets."

Then the people, and especially the children, shouted for joy; but, as soon as there was silence, Charles said to the orange man, " Thank'e, master, with all my heart; but I can't take your oranges, only that one I earned; take the rest back again: as for a black eye, that's nothing! but I won't be paid for it: no more than for doing what's honest. So I can't take your oranges, master; but I thank you as much as if I had them." Saying these words, Charles offered to pour the oranges back into the basket; but the man would not let him.

" Then," said Charles, " if they are honestly mine, I may give them away;" so he emptied the hat amongst the children, his companions. " Divide them amongst you," said he; and without waiting for their thanks, he pressed

through the croud and ran towards
home. The children all followed him,
clapping their hands and thanking him.

The little thief came limping after.
Nobody praised him, nobody thanked
him; he had no oranges to eat, nor had
he any to give away. *People must
be honest before they can be generous.*
Ned sighed, as he went towards home;
" And all this," said he to himself,
" was for one orange; it was not worth
while."

No: it is never worth while to do
wrong.

Little boys, who read this story, consider, which would you rather have
been, *the honest boy*, or *the thief*.

CHERRY ORCHARD.

———◆———

MARIANNE was a little girl of about eight years old; she was remarkably good-tempered; she could bear to be disappointed, or to be contradicted, or to be blamed, without looking or feeling peevish, or sullen, or angry. Her parents, and her school-mistress and companions, all loved her, because she was obedient and obliging.

Marianne had a cousin, a year younger than herself, named Owen, who was an ill-tempered boy; almost every day he was crying, or pouting, or in a passion, about some trifle or other: he was neither obedient nor obliging.

His playfellows could not love him; for he was continually quarrelling with them; he would never, either when he was at play or at work, do what they wished; but he always tried to force them to yield to his will and his humour.

One fine summer's morning, Marianne and Owen were setting out, with several of their little companions, to school. It was a walk of about a mile, from the town in which their fathers and mothers lived, to the school house, if they went by the high-road; but there was another way, through a lane, which was a quarter of a mile shorter.

Marianne, and most of the children, liked to go by the lane, because they could gather the pretty flowers, which grew on the banks, and in the hedges; but Owen preferred going by the high-road, because he liked to see the carts and carriages, and horsemen, which usually were seen upon this road.

Just when they were setting out, Owen called to Marianne, who was turning into the lane.

" Marianne," said he, " you *must* not go by the lane to day; you must go by the road."

" Why must not I go by the lane to day?" said Marianne; " you know, yesterday, and the day before, and the day before that, we all went by the high-road, only to please you; and now let us go by the lane, because we want to gather some honey-suckles and dog-roses, to fill our dame's flower-pots."

" I don't care for that; I don't want to fill our dame's flower-pots; I don't want to gather honey-suckles and dog-roses; I want to see the coaches and chaises on the road; and you *must* go my way, Marianne."

" *Must!* Oh, you should not say *must*," replied Marianne, in a gentle tone.

" No, indeed!" cried one of her companions, you should not; nor should you look so cross: that is not the way to make us do what you like."

" And, besides," said another, " what right has he always to make us do as he pleases? He never will do any thing that we wish."

Owen grew quite angry, when he heard this; and he was just going to make some sharp answer, when Marianne, who was good-natured, and always endeavoured to prevent quarrels, said, " Let us do what he asks, this once; and I dare say he will do what we please the next time—We will go by the high-road to school, and we can come back by the lane, in the cool of the evening."

To please Marianne, whom they all loved, they agreed to this proposal. They went by the high-road; but Owen was not satisfied, because he saw that his companions did not comply for his sake; and, as he walked on, he began to kick up the dust with his feet, saying, " I'm sure it is much pleasanter here than in the lane; I wish we were to come back this way— I'm sure it is much pleasanter here than in the lane; is not it, Marianne ?"

Marianne could not say that she thought so.

Owen kicked up the dust more and more.

" Do not make such a dust, dear Owen," said she; " look how you have covered my shoes and my clean stockings with dust."

" Then say, It is pleasanter here than in the lane.   I shall go on making this dust till you say that."

" I cannot say that, because I do not think so, Owen."

" I'll make you think so and say so too."

" You are not taking the right way to make me think so : you know, that I cannot think this dust agreeable."

Owen persisted : and he raised continually a fresh cloud of dust, in spite of all that Marianne or his companions could say to him.   They left him, and went to the opposite side of the road ; but wherever they went he pursued. At length they came to a turnpike-gate, on one side of which there was a turnstile ; Marianne and the rest of the children passed, one by one, through the turnstile, whilst Owen was emptying his shoes of dust. When this was done, he looked up, and saw all his companions on the other side of the gate, holding the turnstile, to prevent him from coming through.

" Let me through, let me through," cried he; " I must and will come through."

" No, no, Owen," said they, " *must* will not do now; we have you safe; here are ten of us; and we will not let you come through till you have promised that you will not make any more dust."

Owen, without making any answer, began to kick, and push, and pull, and struggle, with all his might; but in vain he struggled, pulled, pushed, and kicked; he found that ten people are stronger than one. When he felt that he could not conquer them by force, he began to cry; and he roared as loud as he possibly could.

No one but the turnpike-man was within hearing; and he stood laughing at Owen.

Owen tried to climb the gate; but he could not get over it, because there were iron spikes at the top.

" Only promise that you will not kick up the dust, and they will let you through," said Marianne.

Owen made no answer, but continued to struggle till his whole face was scarlet, and till both his wrists ached: he could not move the turnstile an inch.

" Well," said he, stopping short, " now you are all of you joined toge-ther, you are stronger than I; but I am as cunning as you."

He left the stile and began to walk homewards.

"Where are you going? You will be too late at school, if you turn back and go by the lane," said Marianne.

"I know that very well: but that will be your fault and not mine—I shall tell our dame, that you all of you held the turnstile against me, and would not let me through."

"And we shall tell our dame why we held the turnstile against you," replied one of the children; "and then it will be plain that it was your fault."

Perhaps Owen did not hear this; for he was now at some distance from the gate. Presently he heard some one running after him—It was Marianne.

"Oh, I am so much out of breath with running after you!—I can hardly speak!—But I am come back," said this good-natured girl, " to tell you, that you will be sorry, if you do not come with us; for there is something that you like very much, just at the turn of the road, a little beyond the turnpike-gate."

" Something that I like very much! —What can that be ? "

" Come with *me*, and you shall *see*," said Marianne : " that is both rhyme and reason—Come with *me*, and you shall *see*."

She looked so good-humoured, as she smiled and nodded at him, that he could not be sullen any longer.

" I don't know how it is, cousin Marianne," said he; " but when I am cross, you are never cross; and you can always bring me back to good-humour again, you are so good-humoured yourself—I wish I was like you—But we

need not talk any more of that now——
What is that I shall see on the other
side of the turnpike-gate? What is it
that I like very much?"

"Don't you like ripe cherries very
much?"

"Yes; but they do not grow in these
hedges."

"No; but there is an old woman
sitting by the road-side, with a board before her, which is covered with red ripe
cherries."

"Red ripe cherries! Let us make
haste then," cried Owen. He ran on, as
fast as he could; but as soon as the
children saw him running, they also began to run back to the turnstile; and
they reached it before he did; and they
held it fast as before, saying, "Promise you will not kick up the dust, or
we will not let you through."

" The cherries are very ripe," said Marianne.

" Well, well, I will not kick up the dust—Let me through," said Owen.

They did so and he kept his word; for, though he was ill-humoured, he was a boy of truth, and he always kept his promises. He found the cherries looked red and ripe, as Marianne had described them.

The old woman took up a long stick, which lay on the board before her. Bunches of cherries were tied with white thread to this stick; and, as she shook it in the air, over the heads of the children, they all looked up with longing eyes.

" A halfpenny a bunch !—Who will buy? Who will buy? Who will buy?— Nice ripe cherries !" cried the old woman.

The children held out their halfpence; and " Give me a bunch!" and " Give me a bunch!" was heard on all sides.

" Here are eleven of you," said the old woman, " and there are just eleven bunches on this stick." She put the stick into Marianne's hand, as she spoke.

Marianne began to untie the bunches; and her companions pressed closer and closer to her, each eager to have the particular bunch which they thought the largest and the ripest.

Several fixed upon the uppermost, which looked indeed extremely ripe.

" You cannot all have this bunch," said Marianne; " to which of you must I give it? You all wish for it."

" Give it to me, give it to *me*," was the first cry of each; but the second was, " Keep it yourself, Marianne; keep it yourself."

" Now, Owen, see what it is to be good-natured, and good-humoured, like Marianne," said William, the eldest of the boys, who stood near him — " We all are ready to give up the ripest cherries to Marianne; but we should never think of doing so for you, because you are so cross and disagreeable."

" I am not cross *now;* I am not disagreeable *now*," replied Owen; " and I do not intend to be cross and disagreeable any more."

This was a good resolution; but Owen did not keep it many minutes. In the bunch of cherries, which Marianne gave to him for his share, there was one which, though red on one side, was entirely white and hard on the other.

" This cherry is not ripe; and here's another that has been half eaten away by the birds. Oh, Marianne, you gave me this bad bunch on purpose—I will not have this bunch."

"Somebody must have it," said William; "and I do not see that it is worse than the others; we shall all have some cherries that are not so good as the rest, but we shall not grumble, and look so cross about it as you do."

"Give me your bad cherries, and I will give you two out of my fine bunch, instead of them," said the good-natured Marianne.

"No, no, no!" cried the children; "Marianne, keep your own cherries."

"Are not you ashamed, Owen?" said William: "How can you be so greedy?"

"Greedy! I am not greedy," cried Owen, angrily; "but I will not have the worst cherries; I will have another bunch."

He tried to snatch another bunch from the stick. William held it above his head. Owen leaped up, reached it; and, when his companions closed round him, exclaiming against his violence, he grew still more angry; he threw the stick down upon the ground, and trampled upon every bunch of the cherries in his fury, scarcely knowing what he did, or what he said.

When his companions saw the ground stained with the red juice of their cherries, which he had trampled under his feet, they were both sorry and angry.

The children had not any more half-pence; they could not buy any more cherries; and the old woman said, that she could not *give* them any.

As they went away sorrowfully, they

said, "Owen is so ill-tempered, that we will not play with him, or speak to him, or have any thing to do with him."

Owen thought, that he could make himself happy without his companions; and he told them so. But he soon found that he was mistaken.

When they arrived at the school-house, their dame was sitting in the thatched porch before her own door, reading a paper that was printed in large letters. —" My dears," said she to her little scholars, " here is something that you will be glad to see; but say your lessons first—One thing at a time; duty first, and pleasure afterwards — Whichever of you says your lesson best, shall know first what is in this paper, and shall have the pleasure of telling the good news."

Owen always learned his lessons very well, and quickly : he now said his lesson better than any of his companions said theirs; and he looked round him with joy and triumph: but no eye met his with pleasure; nobody smiled upon him; no one was glad that he had succeeded: on the contrary, he heard those near him whisper, "I should have been very glad if it had been Marianne, who had said her lesson best, because she is so good-natured."

The printed paper, which Owen read aloud, was as follows:—

"On Thursday evening next, the gate of the cherry orchard will be opened; and all, who have tickets, will be let in, from six o'clock till eight. Price of tickets, sixpence."

The children wished extremely to go to this cherry orchard, where they knew that they might gather as many cherries as they liked, and where they thought that they should be very happy, sitting down under the trees, and eating fruit —But none of these children had any money; for they had spent their last halfpence in paying for those cherries, which they never tasted—those cherries, which Owen, in the fury of his passion, trampled in the dust.

The children asked their dame what they could do to earn sixpence apiece; and she told them, that they might perhaps be able to earn this money by plaiting straw for hats, which they had all been taught to make by their good dame.

Immediately the children desired to set to work.

Owen, who was very eager to go to the cherry orchard, was the most anxious to get forward with the business: he found, however, that nobody liked to

work along with him; his companions
said, " We are afraid that you should
quarrel with us—We are afraid that you
should fly into a passion about the
straws, as you did about the cherries;
therefore we will not work with you."

"Will not you? then I will work by
myself," said Owen; "and I dare say,
that I shall have done my work long
before you have any of you finished
yours; for I can plait quicker and better than any of you."

It was true, that Owen could plait
quicker and better than any of his companions; but he was soon surprised to
find, that his work did not go on so fast
as theirs.

After they had been employed all the
remainder of this evening, and all the
next day, Owen went to his companions,
and compared his work with theirs.

" How is this?" said he; " how comes it, that you have all done so much, and I have not done nearly so much, though I work quicker than any one of you, and I have worked as hard as I possibly could? What is the reason, that you have done so much more than I have?"

" Because we have all been helping one another, and you have had no one to help you: you have been obliged to do every thing for yourself."

" But still, I do not understand how your helping one another can make such a difference," said Owen: " I plait faster than any of you."

His companions were so busy at their work, that they did not listen to what he was saying—He stood behind Marianne, in a melancholy posture, looking at them, and trying to find out why they went on so much faster than he could

—He observed, that one picked the outside off the straws; another cut them to the proper length; another sorted them, and laid them in bundles; another flattened them; another (the youngest of the little girls, who was not able to do any thing else) held the straws ready for those who were plaiting; another cut off the rough ends of the straws when the plaits were finished; another ironed the plaits with a hot smoothing-iron; others sewed the plaits together. Each did what he could do best and quickest; and none of them lost any time in going from one work to another, or in looking for what they wanted.

On the contrary, Owen had lost a great deal of time in looking for all the things that he wanted; he had nobody to hold the straws ready for him as he plaited; therefore, he was forced to go

2 A 3

for them himself, every time he wanted them; and his straws were not sorted in nice bundles for him; the wind blew them about; and he wasted half an hour, at least, in running after them. Besides this, he had no friend to cut off the rough ends for him; nor had he any one to sew the plaits together; and though he could plait quickly, he could not sew quickly; for he was not used to this kind of work. He wished extremely for Marianne to do it for him. He was once a full quarter of an hour in threading his needle, of which the eye was too small—Then he spent another quarter of an hour in looking for one with a larger eye; and he could not find it at last, and nobody would lend him another—When he had done sewing, he found, that *his hand was out for plaiting:* that is, he could not plait so quickly after his fingers had just been used to another kind of work; and when he had been smoothing the straws with a heavy iron, his hand trembled afterwards for some minutes, during which time he was forced to be idle; thus it was, that he lost time, by doing every thing for himself; and though he lost but a few minutes or seconds in each particular, yet, when all these minutes and seconds were added together, they made a great difference.

" How fast, how very fast they go on! and how merrily!" said Owen, as he looked at his former companions—" I am sure I shall never earn sixpence for myself before Thursday; and I shall not be able to go to the cherry-orchard —I am very sorry, that I trampled on your cherries; I am very sorry, that I was so ill-humoured—I will never be cross any more."

" He is very sorry, that he was so ill-humoured; he is very sorry, that he trampled on our cherries," cried Marianne; " Do you hear what he says? he will never be cross any more."

" Yes, we hear what he says," answered William; " but how are we to be sure that he will do as he says?"

" Oh," cried another of his companions, " he has found out at last, that he must do as he would be done by."

" Aye," said another; " and he finds, that we, who are good-humoured and good-natured to one another do better even than he, who is so quick and so clever."

" But if, besides being so quick and so clever, he was good-humoured and good-natured," said Marianne, " he would be of great use to us; he plaits a vast deal faster than Mary does, and

Mary plaits faster than any of us—
Come, let us try him, let him come in
amongst us."

" No, no, no," cried many voices;
" he will quarrel with us; and we have
no time for quarrelling—We are all so
quiet and so happy without him ! Let
him work by himself, as he said he
would."

Owen went on, working by himself:
he made all the haste that he possibly
could; but Thursday came, and his
work was not nearly finished—His companions passed by him with their finished work in their hands—Each, as they
passed, said, " What, have not you done
yet, Owen ?" and then they walked on
to the table where their dame was sitting ready to pay them their sixpences.

She measured their work, and examined it; and, when she saw that it was

well done, she gave to each of her little workmen and workwomen the sixpence which they had earned; and she said, " I hope, my dears, that you will be happy this evening."

They all looked joyful; and, as they held their sixpences in their hands, they said, " If we had not helped one another, we should not have earned this money; and we should not be able to go to the cherry orchard."

" Poor Owen," whispered Marianne to her companions, " look how melancholy he is, sitting there alone at his work! See! his hands tremble, so that he can scarcely hold the straws; he will not have nearly finished his work in time, he cannot go with us."

" He should not have trampled upon our cherries; and then, perhaps, we might have helped him," said William.

" Let us help him, though he did trample on our cherries," said the good-natured Marianne—" He is sorry for what he did, and he will never be so ill-humoured or ill-natured again— Come, let us go and help him— If we all help, we shall have his work finished in time, and then we shall all be happy together."

As Marianne spoke, she drew William near to the corner where Owen was sitting; and all her companions followed.

" Before we offer to help him, let us try whether he is now inclined to be good-humoured and good-natured."

" Yes, yes, let us try that first," said his companions.

" Owen, you will not have done time enough to go with us," said William.

" No, indeed," said Owen, " I shall not; therefore, I may as well give up all thoughts of it—It is my own fault, I know."

" Well, but as you cannot go yourself, you will not want your pretty little basket; will you lend it to us to hold our cherries?"

" Yes, I will, with pleasure," cried Owen, jumping up to fetch it.

" Now he is good-natured, I am sure," said Marianne.

" This plaiting of yours is not nearly so well done as ours," said William; " look how uneven it is."

" Yes, it is rather uneven, indeed," replied Owen.

William began to untwist some of Owen's work; and Owen bore this trial of his patience with good temper.

" Oh, you are pulling it all to pieces, William," said Marianne ; " this is not fair."

" Yes, it is fair," said William, " for I have undone only an inch ; and I will do as many inches for Owen as he pleases, now that I see he is good-humoured."

Marianne immediately sat down to work for Owen; and William and all his companions followed her example — It was now two hours before the time when the cherry orchard was to be opened ; and, during these two hours, they went on so expeditiously, that they completed the work.

Owen went with them to the cherry orchard, where they spent the evening all together very happily — As he was sitting under a tree with his companions, eating the ripe cherries, he said to them

—" Thank you all for helping me; I should not have been here now eating these ripe cherries, if you had not been so good-natured to me—I hope I shall never be cross to any of you again; whenever I feel inclined to be cross, I will think of your good-nature to me, and of THE CHERRY ORCHARD."

END OF VOL. I.

CHARLES WOOD, Printer,
Poppin's Court, Fleet Street, London.

Correct List of Mr. and Miss Edgeworth's Works.

RATIONAL PRIMER, by Mr. Edgeworth.

EARLY LESSONS FOR CHILDREN, in 2 vols.

CONTINUATION OF EARLY LESSONS, in 2 vols.

PARENT'S ASSISTANT; or, Stories for Children, 6 vols.

POETRY EXPLAINED FOR THE USE OF YOUNG PEOPLE, by Mr. Edgeworth.

READINGS IN POETRY, by Mr. Edgeworth.

ESSAYS ON PRACTICAL EDUCATION, by Mr. and Miss Edgeworth, 2 vols.

PROFESSIONAL EDUCATION, by Mr. Edgeworth.

LETTERS FOR LITERARY LADIES.

CASTLE RACKRENT, an Hibernian Tale.

ESSAY ON IRISH BULLS, by Mr. and Miss Edgeworth.

MORAL TALES, 3 vols.

BELINDA, 3 vols.

LEONORA, 2 vols.

THE MODERN GRISELDA.

POPULAR TALES, 3 vols.

TALES OF FASHIONABLE LIFE, 6 vols.

PATRONAGE, 4 vols.

COMIC DRAMAS, 12mo.

HARRINGTON, and ORMOND, Tales, 3 vols., 12mo.

ESSAY ON THE CONSTRUCTION OF ROADS AND CARRIAGES, by Mr. Edgeworth.

The following are also published by BALDWIN, CRADOCK, and JOY; and R. HUNTER.

By Mrs. BARBAULD and Dr. AIKIN.

1. EVENINGS AT HOME; or, THE JUVENILE BUDGET OPENED: consisting of a Variety of Miscellaneous Pieces, for the Instruction and Amusement of Young Persons. In 6 vols., half-bound, price 10s. 6d.

2. LESSONS FOR CHILDREN, from Two to Four Years of Age. In Four Parts, price 9d. each, or 3s. 6d. bound together.

3. HYMNS IN PROSE, for Children. 16th edition, enlarged and much improved, price 1s. 6d.

4. ARTS OF LIFE:—1. Of Providing Food; 2. Of Providing Clothing; 3. Of Providing Shelter:—described in a Series of Letters, for the Instruction of Young Persons. Half-bound, price 2s. 6d.

Elementary Books for Youth, lately published.

5. THE FEMALE SPEAKER: or, Miscellaneous Pieces, in Prose and Verse: selected from the best Writers, and adapted to the Use of Young Women. In 18mo, price, bound, 5s.

6. NATURAL HISTORY OF THE YEAR, being an Enlargement of the Calendar of Nature. By Mr. ARTHUR AIKIN, 12mo, 9s. bound.

7. JUVENILE CORRESPONDENCE; or, Letters designed as Examples of the Epistolary Style, for Children of both Sexes. By MISS AIKIN, 12mo, half-bound, 2s. 6d.

By the Rev. J. JOYCE.

1. SCIENTIFIC DIALOGUES; intended for the Instruction and Entertainment of Young People: in which the First Principles of Natural and Experimental Philosophy are fully explained. In 6 vols., 15s. half-bd.; comprising Mechanics, Astronomy, Hydrostatics, Pneumatics, Optics and Magnetism, Electricity and Galvanism.

2. A COMPANION to the SCIENTIFIC DIALOGUES; or, The Tutor's Assistant and Pupil's Manual in Natural and Experimental Philosophy; containing a complete Set of Questions and other Exercises, for the Examination of Pupils in the Scientific Dialogues, and forming a Seventh Volume of that Work. Half-bound, 2s. 6d.

3. DIALOGUES ON CHEMISTRY, intended for the Instruction and Entertainment of Young People; in which the First Principles of that Science are fully explained; with Questions and other Exercises for the Examination of Pupils. In 2 vols., price, half-bound, 7s.

4. LETTERS on Natural and Experimental Philosophy, Chemistry, Anatomy, Physiology, and other branches of Science pertaining to the Material World. Illustrated with 19 Plates, 12mo, boards, 10s. 6d.

5. DIALOGUES ON THE MICROSCOPE, intended for the Instruction and Entertainment of Young Persons desirous of investigating the Wonders of the minuter parts of the Creation. With ten Plates, in 2 vols. 12mo, price 7s. half-bound.

6. CATECHISM OF NATURE, improved and enlarged. The tenth edition, price 1s. 6d.

" Read Nature, Nature is a Friend to Truth."

YOUNG.

Trieste

Trieste Publishing has a massive catalogue of classic book titles. Our aim is to provide readers with the highest quality reproductions of fiction and non-fiction literature that has stood the test of time. The many thousands of books in our collection have been sourced from libraries and private collections around the world.

The titles that Trieste Publishing has chosen to be part of the collection have been scanned to simulate the original. Our readers see the books the same way that their first readers did decades or a hundred or more years ago. Books from that period are often spoiled by imperfections that did not exist in the original. Imperfections could be in the form of blurred text, photographs, or missing pages. It is highly unlikely that this would occur with one of our books. Our extensive quality control ensures that the readers of Trieste Publishing's books will be delighted with their purchase. Our staff has thoroughly reviewed every page of all the books in the collection, repairing, or if necessary, rejecting titles that are not of the highest quality. This process ensures that the reader of one of Trieste Publishing's titles receives a volume that faithfully reproduces the original, and to the maximum degree possible, gives them the experience of owning the original work.

We pride ourselves on not only creating a pathway to an extensive reservoir of books of the finest quality, but also providing value to every one of our readers. Generally, Trieste books are purchased singly - on demand, however they may also be purchased in bulk. Readers interested in bulk purchases are invited to contact us directly to enquire about our tailored bulk rates. Email: customerservice@triestepublishing.com

You May Also Like

ISBN: 9780649731213
Paperback: 160 pages
Dimensions: 6.14 x 0.34 x 9.21 inches
Language: eng

War Poems, 1898

California Club & Irving M. Scott

ISBN: 9780649565733
Paperback: 170 pages
Dimensions: 6.14 x 0.36 x 9.21 inches
Language: eng

Longmans' English Classics; Dryden's Palamon and Arcite

William Tenney Brewster

www.triestepublishing.com

You May Also Like

Hour by Hour; Or, The Christian's Daily Life

E. A. L.

ISBN: 9780649607242
Paperback: 172 pages
Dimensions: 6.14 x 0.37 x 9.21 inches
Language: eng

The Lost Found, and the Wanderer Welcomed

W. M. Taylor

ISBN: 9780649639663
Paperback: 188 pages
Dimensions: 6.14 x 0.40 x 9.21 inches
Language: eng

www.triestepublishing.com

You May Also Like

ISBN: 9780649420544
Paperback: 108 pages
Dimensions: 6.14 x 0.22 x 9.21 inches
Language: eng

1807-1907 The One Hundredth Anniversary of the incorporation of the Town of Arlington Massachusetts

Various

ISBN: 9780649194292
Paperback: 44 pages
Dimensions: 6.14 x 0.09 x 9.21 inches
Language: eng

Biennial report of the Board of State Harbor Commissioners, for the two fiscal years commencing July 1, 1890, and ending June 30, 1892

Various

You May Also Like

Biennial report of the Board of State Harbor Commissioners for the two fisca years. Commeneing July 1, 1884, and Ending June 30, 1886

Various

Biennial report of the Board of state commissioners, for the two fiscal years, commencing July 1, 1890, and ending June 30, 1892

Various

Find more of our titles on our website. We have a selection of thousands of titles that will interest you. Please visit

www.triestepublishing.com

Lightning Source UK Ltd.
Milton Keynes UK
UKOW06f0944231017
311488UK00005B/949/P